Inspect

Breaks an Egg

INSPECTOR GHOTE
Breaks an Egg

H.R.F. KEATING

Academy
Chicago
Publishers

Published in 1985 by

Academy Chicago Publishers
425 N. Michigan Ave.
Chicago, Illinois 60611

Published by arrangement with
Doubleday & Co.

Copyright © 1970 by
H.R.F. Keating

Printed and bound in the U.S.A.

Library of Congress Cataloging-in-Publication Data
Keating, H. R. F. (Henry Reymond Fitzwalter), 1926–.
    Inspector Ghote breaks an egg.

    I.   Title.
[PR6061.E26I37   1985]   823'.914   85-18519
ISBN 0-89733-177-X (pbk.)

1

Inspector Ghote nearly broke his eggs before he had been in the little town two minutes.

He was leaving the station in a hurry, determined, despite his weariness after a long night in the train from Bombay and despite the onset of yet another heavy shower of steamy rain in this end-of-monsoon period, not to waste an unnecessary moment before seizing hold of the slippery-seeming facts of his task.

From the moment that he had been landed with the business only the afternoon before, he had raged at the lack of anything he could get his teeth into, and now that the chance was near he was going to let nothing delay him.

He had been cosily immersed in paperwork in the warren of Bombay CID Headquarters with all the familiar objects of his stuffy little office comforting him – his desk whose every scored line and varnish whorl he knew and loved, the narrow brass tray in which he kept his pencils, the non-issue set of bamboo-edged shelves with its screwed-on plastic labels saying 'Songs', 'Dance', 'Piano', 'Sacred' and 'Various' and, above all, in its place of honour on top of these shelves, Hans Gross's *Criminal Investigation*, mildew-stained but masterly. And then the summons had violently broken into his peace.

First, Deputy Superintendent Samant had jerked open the door and barked at him to be ready to receive a telephone call from 'an eminent figure in our public life'. And hardly had the DSP gone, with a parting warning that the call would mean dropping all other work for an indefinite period, coupled with a sharp request to supply him with his criminal statistics 'without delay', when the call from the Eminent Figure himself had come.

The orders Ghote had received from him, though well

wrapped up, were simple enough. Fifteen years ago, he had been told, the wife of an ambitious young politician in a distant town near the State border had died quite suddenly in extremely suspicious circumstances. And soon afterwards the rising politician had married the only child of the Chairman of the town's Municipal Council, to inherit within a year a considerable fortune and, what was more important, considerable local influence. He in his turn was now Municipal Chairman and had ten thousand votes depending on his word alone.

Very little appeared to have been done to investigate the first wife's fatal illness at the time, the Eminent Figure had said.

It was only when he went on to mention that this same Municipal Chairman had recently been so incredibly foolish as to abandon his long-held political allegiance that Ghote had begun to realize what lay in store for him: an investigation fifteen years old with one suspect only, a man vested with something like absolute powers in his own domain, and a result, one result only, to be obtained as quickly as possible. It was a decidedly tricky business.

And the trickiness of the whole affair was what accounted for Ghote arriving in the little town with the eggs.

They were a dozen fresh eggs, quite extraordinary in size, and they reposed, each preserved in a layer of smearily shining grease, in a soft cardboard box of a glaring orange colour with bold blue lettering all across it: 'Grofat Chicken Feeds Pvt. Ltd'.

The Eminent Figure had been responsible.

'I have given some thought to the guise in which you should go about when you get there tomorrow,' he had said. 'It would be best for as few people as possible to know of your mission.'

Ghote had promised his wife and small son to take them next day to see a certain smash-hit film, 'the greatest suspense thriller the screen has ever seen – 23rd colourful week – set to haunting music', and now he would have to catch a train before night fell.

'You will go,' the Eminent Figure had continued silkily, 'under the appearance of a salesman, a salesman for a new chicken-feed product. The average size of the Indian egg, did you know, is disgraceful as compared with the American and

6

the British egg. It is nothing less, indeed, than a national disaster.'

He had left such a pause at this that Ghote had felt obliged to speak.

'Yes, sir, I have no doubt.'

'Now it so happens that a young nephew of mine has recently purchased a mill for the manufacture of a product guaranteed to increase the size of an egg by as much as forty per cent, and I have been able to secure for you one of the samples with which he equips his salesmen. I will have it dispatched to CID Headquarters immediately. It will be exactly what you require.'

'Yes, sir. Thank you.'

Ghote had rejected the notion of explaining to the Eminent Figure that, although within a reasonable distance of Bombay there were egg farms, often run as a hobby by wealthy film-stars, in the remote part of the state to which he was being sent chickens were just one more set of scavengers feeding where they could on what they could find.

After all, one did have a duty to look after one's family. There could be no gainsaying that.

But he hoped profoundly, now that he had arrived, that the disguise the bold orange box provided would be sufficient.

In front of him as he paused in the station entrance there stretched a large area of nondescript muddy ground, diversified by huge puddles which heavy drops of rain were converting into so many miniature boiling and bubbling lakes. A big tamarind tree stood about thirty yards away to one side with a sad-looking hut of a shop near it, now apparently deserted. To the other side, the road leading into the main part of the town began an uncertain existence. Just at the point where it finally made up its mind it would have to be a road after all there was a small tamarind tree and under its doubtful shelter two tongas waited, the tonga-wallas hunched over their dashboards looking down at ribby horses with coloured head-plumes drooping sadly in the damp and the heat.

Ghote fixed his eyes on them and prepared to run across and take the first that offered.

And, at the very moment he started out, it happened. A miserable-looking figure whom he had scarcely noticed crouching beside him in the station entrance took it into its head to go forth into the world at that same instant, and Ghote tripped near-sprawlingly over a foot or a knee or an elbow. For a second he skeltered over the much-trodden muddy ground outside the station entrance, with the thought vivid in his mind just how furious the Eminent Figure would be if it ever came out that a box of extra large eggs prominently labelled with the name of his nephew's firm had been smashed to sticky fragments within minutes of their arrival at their destination.

In the end he saved them and stood, his heart thudding and the heavy rain splashing copiously over him, trying to regain the determined calm he had possessed only moments before.

He turned to see what or when or whom it was that he had stumbled over.

It was an old woman, a hopeless wretched outcaste creature, dressed in a sari that must once have been gaudy indeed but was now through years of wear reduced to the drabness of dust. She was scrabbling to her feet, a look of venomous rage on her scimitar-nosed face with its scattering of thick curly grey hairs randomly sprouting.

She must have been travelling on the train, Ghote thought.

All her possessions were with her, half in an enormous glass jar – which once, according to its still intact label, had contained 'Ovax the Egg Drink of the Night' – and half in an earthenware pot that had been tipped over by the collision between them and had had most of its contents scattered over the slimy, foot-trodden mud.

But the crone, when she had recovered herself, ignored them all in favour of hobbling, spitting curses all the way, after an unexpectedly clean-looking copy of a magazine that she had, for what reasons it was hard to conceive, been clutching in one hand.

It had been blown by a puff of wind, or even forced over the ground by the battering raindrops, to within a foot or two of Ghote himself. He stooped and picked it up, wondering as he did so whether in a place as remote and old-fashioned as this he would get into trouble for having so much contact with a harijan woman. In towns of this sort the old ways were still powerful.

'Mine, mine,' the old crone crackled at him.

'Yes, yes, I am giving,' he answered, arranging the flapping pages as he spoke.

And then, a couple of words in the precious magazine caught his eye and quite transfixed him with astonishment.

There in bold black letters in the middle of a narrow column of print was his own name.

It was quite clear, unmistakable. 'Ghote Goes In'. And the paragraph read on: 'Top trouble-shooter Inspector Ganesh Ghote (pronounced Gotay) of Bombay CID is to be sent ... '

Totally ignoring in his utter surprise the old crone, who was by now plucking at his shirt sleeve, he looked up at the top of the page to see what on earth magazine it was that for some unimaginable reason was writing about him.

It was *Time. Time* magazine. He knew it. He had seen DSP Samant reading it.

But why? Why his name in *Time*?

He scurried to the head of the article. 'Saint-v-CID'. What was this? He read at lightning speed.

There was not, when he conducted one heat-stroke of analysis on the piece, all that much to it. Facts were evidently hard to come by. But what there were were terrible. The piece dealt precisely with the case he had just at this moment arrived to tackle, but it added one item that he had had no idea of. It seemed that a local holy man had, for unexplained reasons, set his face against the whole investigation into the Municipal Chairman's first wife's death. He was conducting a fast against any further inquiries, a fast 'unto death'. And he had already been doing so for forty-eight days 'as of now'. There was a picture too, not of the 'saint' nor of the 'CID man' – and thank heavens for that at least – but of the Municipal Chairman, a sharp, crocodile-grinning face under a narrow white Congress cap, a good photograph, crystal clear, even down to a birthmark on the chin. 'Chairman Savarkar: A Swami's protection'.

A sudden whip-like fury sprang up in Ghote's mind against

9

the Eminent Figure who had so cunningly briefed him the day before. There had been not the least mention of this trouble. And it must have been well enough known about in this area for some sharp-eyed correspondent to have got hold of the tale and sent it as an amusing story – an amusing story – to *Time* magazine. And, worse, it had already been decided then, days and days ago, that he himself was to be sent to investigate. He had been the last to be told.

He was standing facing the station entrance. He very nearly marched straight back in and demanded the time of the next train to Bombay.

How could he conduct a tricky business of this sort when the whole town would be expecting him? When they all knew that he had been sent here to make out a case against Vinayak Savarkar, the man among them all who could see to it in the twinkling of an eye that any local official who came under his displeasure was moved off the scene for ever, who could do a thousand and one useful things for anybody who had obliged him, from getting a place for a boy at a coveted school to acquiring reserved train seats at a moment's notice? What hope would there be of getting admissions about any dubious conduct fifteen years ago out of the people already warned in this way?

The hand pluck-plucking at his shirt became yet more insistent. The sprouting-haired face looking up into his was contorted with anxiety and anger.

'Sahib, it is mine, mine. I must have, Sahib.'

He thrust the wretched magazine into the crone's hand and watched her hobble away, clutching, one in either wrinkled arm, her earthenware pot and her Ovax jar.

Then he turned and set out for the waiting tongas. After all, he had been given orders, he had to obey.

So, with as an addition to his troubles the extreme slowness of the ride into the centre of the sleepy and stifling little town, and the continuing downpour which while it lasted sent spouts of water in through the unmended rents in the hood of the tonga, Ghote was feeling more despondent than determined when he reached the main street.

It lay, he saw, wide and puddle-pocked, with occasional

bullock-carts and cyclists proceeding along it and some determinedly browsing cows, squatting children and rummaging pidogs scattered here and there, not to mention two hostages to the spirit of modernity in the shape of parked motor-cars, one dilapidated to the point of ruin and the other by contrast overwhelmingly bulbous and glossy.

But then at last there was the police-station, standing heavily whitewashed in every particular, between the Palace Talkies – now showing the last record-breaking hit film Ghote had succeeded in taking his wife to in Bombay about a year before – and on the other side of Rao Dispensary (Dr R. Rao: propr). And, as the tonga began to slow yet more its already leaden pace, Ghote greeted the smartness of the building with a small lifting of the spirit.

Policemen were policemen everywhere.

And then, when he had already risen in the tonga's rearward-facing seat balancing the burdensome orange egg-box on his widespread right palm, the vehicle suddenly lurched sharply forward.

It was all he could do, clutching desperately at its frail side with his one free hand, to keep himself in at all. And in a couple of seconds he found himself clacking along the wide street again at a speed quite twice that which the lean-shanked horse had attained at any point in the journey before.

He jockeyed the egg-box on to the patched leather seat behind him and heaved himself down beside it. He was in the process of swivelling round to give the tongawalla a furious reprimand when the vehicle was pulled to a shakingly abrupt halt right in front of the big bulbous parked car.

A man in a white Gandhi cap was leaning out of its back window, a cigar clamped between widely grinning teeth. Ghote recognized him instantly, if only because of the big blotchy birthmark in the shape of a well-prowed boat on his lower left jaw. It was the Municipal Chairman.

And at once Ghote understood what had happened to his tongawalla. The fellow had not simply been struck with a fit of total wilfulness. When his vehicle had jerked forward in that startling way it had been because Vinayak Savarkar had

11

leant out of the window of his big car and had beckoned. When the Municipal Chairman beckoned in this town people came running.

And then to Ghote's sheer astonishment the Chairman, removing for an instant the long cigar from his grinning teeth, actually addressed him by name.

'It is Inspector Ghote? From Bombay, all the way?'

Ghote looked at him in mute fury.

How on earth had the man known that this perfectly ordinary looking chap in white shirt and trousers sitting in an ordinary station tonga was an inspector of the Bombay CID?

'You are wondering how I know that you are the famous Inspector Ghote, long stories in the newspapers?' the Municipal Chairman asked now with another snapping grin.

'No,' Ghote shouted.

'But you are Inspector Ghote?'

Ghote swiftly considered denying it.

'I see you are wondering whether to deny,' the Chairman said. 'But I am telling you it would be of no use whatsoever. I know too much.'

He sucked at the end of his cigar like a street-boy sucking at the end of a piece of sugar cane, with concentrated fervour.

'So you are wondering still? Yes? No?'

He actually waited for Ghote's answer.

'Yes,' Ghote said with dignity, sitting straighter on the tonga's worn seat. 'Yes, I am wondering.'

'It is very simple,' the Chairman answered, with something of the air of a very intelligent teacher instructing a provenly dull pupil. 'A certain Eminent Figure in Bombay may send his spies to this town, but he forgets that I can send my spies to him. And no sooner had Inspector Ghote boarded the train at VT Station last night than a good friend of mine telephoned me straightaway. So when that train arrives at our town and I see just one of the station tongas coming I am not in much difficulty knowing who is here.'

'Very well then,' Ghote said, realizing with a glint of reviving guile that at least the boldly labelled egg-box was down on the tonga seat out of sight, 'very well, I have come. I have come on orders to investigate the death of your late wife and I mean to carry out that investigation.'

The Chairman threw his cigar down into the slushy mud of the street. It was smoked to half its length only.

'Now then, Inspector Ghote,' he said, 'shall I tell you why I went to such trouble to make sure I saw you just as soon as you were arriving?'

'If you like,' Ghote said.

The lean horse in the shafts of the tonga took a sudden half-step forward in an effort to get hold of a strip of much-trodden mango peel. The frail vehicle swayed and swung on its single axle. Ghote grabbed both sides.

He saw the Chairman's wide mouth snap up the incident like a gecko lizard snapping up a chance mosquito.

'Well then, Inspector, I did it so as to give you good advice. Good advice while there was still plenty of time for you. It is this: in Bombay things may be different but in this town it is what I say that goes. I am boss, see? I am telling you, every single damn one of the officials in this town owes his place to me – the District Judge, the Superintending Engineer, the Number One at the Hospital, the Head of the Public Works Department, the House Rents Controller – all, all. So ask who you want, ask what you want, you will not be learning one damn thing. See?'

His wide grin flashed out at Ghote, hard as a barrier of white-coated steel.

'Now,' he went on with unabated cheerfulness, 'I am a reasonable man, Inspector. I know you have been given a job to do, and you must do it. So you stay in the town. Do not go. Enjoy yourself.'

His eyes flicked over the street.

'Go to the Palace Talkies,' he said, 'No need to pay, just give your name to Manager. I will see he is informed. Best seat every night. And afterwards just drop in at the Krishna Bhavan Restaurant, or, if you do not like, try the Royal Hindu. Both proprietors are very good friends of mine. They will make no charge.'

He pushed his head a little further out of the car window,

happily ignoring the few drops of rain that still fell at the tail end of the shower.

'Oh, Inspector,' he said with an atrocious wink, 'if it is a matter of gay girls. It is Francis Street you are wanting. Do not mind which house. Of all I am landlord. Just to give my name. And then when you have stayed week, or ten days even, back to Bombay you go and tell them no bloody good. All right?'

The head went back in at the car window. The window began to rise.

'No,' Ghote shouted, causing the tonga to rock violently once more. 'No. It is not all right.'

Abruptly the window was lowered to its full depth.

The chairman's grin shot out from it like a whip-crack.

'But listen, Inspector, also,' he said. 'It is not top men only that are my friends in this town. There are goondas too that I know. Bad hats, Inspector, every one of them. Men who would not hesitate to set upon a perfectly innocent man in the street at night and beat the daylights out from him.'

Ghote stood bolt upright still in the gently oscillating tonga.

'I am a police officer,' he said.

That and no more.

2

The Municipal Chairman did not appear to be greatly put out by Ghote's declaration. Yet perhaps his flashing grin was a little subdued as he slowly wound up the window of his big car muttering 'As you like, as you like.' And when the gross vehicle squelched slowly forward through the slush and wide puddles of the street Ghote was able to see that the birth-marked face on the far side of the glass was looking decidedly thoughtful.

He felt pretty thoughtful himself.

He had known from the start that he would not be able to conduct an investigation in a place like this without tough opposition. But somehow the very openness with which the Chairman had laid down his cards made the difficulties ahead seem all the more mountainous.

No doubt there had been some boasting in what had been said. A District Judge was hardly likely to be completely in the man's pocket. And probably too most of the other officials whose names had been rattled off like that were not so indebted to him as he had made out. But, on the other hand, it was perfectly certain that anyone as rich as Vinayak Savarkar could have plenty of goondas at his beck and call. And he could see to it that they got away with inflicting a beating-up, too. There would be plenty of lawyers ready to discover something to the discredit of the arresting officer in such a case, or to invent it.

And when such a person as the Municipal Chairman also had the backing of the forces of good, as it seemed, in the shape of a holy man prepared to fast for days and days in order to protect him from any investigation, then the outlook was black indeed.

Ghote clambered down from the tonga and took some satisfaction in paying the driver the very minimum fare. Then, doing his best to conceal the gaudy egg-box in his cradling arms while it could still be linked with the Inspector Ghote the Chairman had spoken to, he picked his way back down the muddy street to the police-station.

If that man is not to get away with it every time, he thought to himself, there is only one thing for it. I must just act so damn quickly that even he is not prepared for me.

Inside the police-station the comforting impression Ghote had gained from its exterior smartness was at once reinforced. The outer office was in a state of scrubbed cleanliness on every scrubbable surface and everything that could possibly be polished had been polished till it dazzled. The constables on duty were every one turned out to a nicety, down to the last neat fold in their turbans.

One of them came smartly forward when Ghote presented himself at the uncluttered wooden counter, and when Ghote, in a careful undertone, gave him his name, there was an immediate and alert reaction.

'Oh, yes, sahib. Special orders from Superintendent Chavan. You are to be taken in to see him *ek dum.*'

Ghote felt a positive stream of warmth go through him. He was on home ground.

He followed the man down a corridor – scrupulously painted doors, each with a clean name-card in a glintingly polished brass holder – and into the interior of the building. Soon the constable stopped, tapped respectfully on a final door, listened for the barked *'Koi hai?'* and spoke up smartly in answer.

'Inspector Ghote, Superintendent sahib. Brought straight in as per orders.'

An instant later the door in front of them was jerked open and Superintendent Chavan stood there.

He was a big man, out-topping Ghote by a good eight inches. Though heavy of build and broad and a little puffy of face, any unpolicemanlike impression this might have made was totally effaced by the extreme correctness of his uniform. It had been ironed to the last rigidity, a very ideal of what its wearer should look like.

While the constable threw up a heel-crashing salute, the superintendent urged Ghote into the office, a broad smile on his broad face.

'Sit down, my dear Inspector, sit down. You smoke?'

A brilliantly polished brass cigarette-box was thrust forward. Ghote seated himself on the chair drawn up dead square to the broad desk.

'It is most kind,' he said. 'But I do not smoke.'

'No? Sensible fellow. Wish I could cure myself of the wretched habit.'

Superintendent Chavan drew up his own well-padded chair with businesslike briskness. He reached forward and adjusted the position of his braided uniform cap that lay to one side of the neatly-kept desk.

'My dear fellow,' he said, 'I cannot tell you how damned pleased I am to see you.'

'I am certainly pleased to be here,' Ghote said.

Superintendent Chavan looked up in surprise.

'Pleased to be here?' he asked. 'In this town? Now?'

Ghote smiled a little ruefully.

'No, not exactly that,' he admitted. 'But I am certainly pleased to be inside a police-station, and such a well-ordered one.'

The superintendent puffed out his broad chest a little.

'I like to think I know how a station should be run, even though we are miles and miles from you chaps in Bombay,' he said.

'It looks so well run that I am a little surprised it was thought necessary to send me here at all,' Ghote replied.

Superintendent Chavan tapped thoughtfully with long fingers on the edge of his braided cap.

'Yes,' he said. 'That is the problem.'

He gave the cap a final little pat, as though he derived strength from it, and continued.

'Perhaps you have not altogether appreciated, my dear Inspector, what it is like to live in a town like this. It is not Bombay, you know. We are not very up to date. You will not find women in slacks, and inter-caste marriages. And here also we have to acknowledge that a certain individual is undoubtedly the boss.'

This confirmation of the words of that 'certain individual' himself struck chilly on Ghote's renewed optimism.

'Boss he may be,' he said, in a defiant attempt to perk himself up. 'But he is not above law.'

'Certainly not, certainly not,' replied the superintendent. 'I hope you did not think I was meaning that.'

Ghote felt the warmth beginning to flow back. At least there was complete solidarity within the police camp, however strong the pressures from outside.

'No,' he said, 'I could see from the moment I entered your station here that there was no question of that sort of thing.'

The superintendent bestowed on his braided cap a little tap of congratulation.

'However,' he said, 'grave problems nevertheless exist. Picture this town, my dear Inspector. We are a little society, in many ways cut off from everywhere else. We have our workers in our

17

cotton mills and our ginning factories, etcetera. And we have our higher reaches of society. Our professional men, our men of wealth. But – and this is my point, my dear Inspector – there are not so many of us here.'

'And so you all know each other well?' Ghote said.

The superintendent wagged his head in vigorous agreement.

'Precisely, precisely. That is exactly it.'

His long fingers stretched out towards the cap again, but desisted inches away.

'So, you see,' he went on, 'it was not easy for me to conduct an investigation myself into a possible crime committed by the leading figure in the little group to which I belong, as it was not easy for my predecessor fifteen years ago – now dead and gone, poor fellow.'

He raised a large palm.

'Not that I myself have flinched from carrying out inquiries since they had to be made,' he said. 'But where could I get? I could question the person we are talking of, certainly. Most rigorously I could question. But I would get nowhere, and then I would need to put questions also to the people he knows. How about that, eh?'

'You would be up against great difficulties questioning your own friends, and they would do their best to hinder you from making things difficult for their friend,' Ghote said.

'I could not have put it better myself, Inspector.'

Superintendent Chavan puffed out a long sigh.

'So that is why I am glad you are able to conduct the investigation henceforth,' he said. 'Frankly, I felt myself tied at every turn.'

Ghote wondered, too, how much the superintendent had felt himself restrained by the presence of the fasting holy man. But he foresaw decided difficulties in broaching such a subject.

'It is not going to be easy work for me,' he began tentatively.

'No, my dear Inspector, I know well that it is not. But rest assured of one thing, any assistance I can give as one police officer to another I will give to my level best.'

Ghote straightened his shoulders and sat more upright.

Perhaps he would wait to find out for himself just how

effective the holy man's crusade was being before he tried to mention the matter. The sense of comradeship he felt with the superintendent was not lightly to be broken.

'Yes,' he said, 'there is much you could do. I was giving the matter consideration in the train last night. I did not sleep very well.'

'And what is this we can do?' Superintendent Chavan said, reaching out to his cap again.

'There must be a Case Diary of the matter from fifteen years ago,' Ghote replied. 'Can you find that for me? And there would be other material also, reports of interviews, a carbon copy of the First Information Report and much else.'

'But these are reports only of what was done fifteen years ago,' the superintendent objected.

And Ghote felt a little spurt of triumph. Here was confirmation that Bombay experience was worth something. No one here had conceived of the possibilities that might lie in these old papers but he was certain he would not get to the end of them without finding something of use.

'I would need to read them all over, every single one,' he said firmly. 'A really thorough check would almost certainly reveal something that has been missed.'

The superintendent looked more than a little crestfallen.

'I can see this was a matter I ought to have had put in hand already,' he said. 'But I will make certain now that every scrap of paper in connection with the case is ready for you first thing tomorrow.'

'No,' said Ghote.

'No?'

'I will begin work now,' Ghote said, rising to his feet.

'But, my dear Inspector, already you have said that you slept little in the train last night. A good hearty meal, an hour or two of rest, and then perhaps a start could be made today.'

'No,' said Ghote obstinately. 'I wish to begin at once.'

The superintendent sighed and picked his cap up off the desk. He put it on and went over to a mirror hanging by the door to make sure it was squarely on his head.

'Very well, my dear fellow,' he said. 'If you are insisting I will see what can be done. But we are faced with a problem here, I do not mind telling.'

'What is this?' Ghote asked, with some sharpness.

'It is a question of accommodation, my dear fellow. Tomorrow by a stroke of good luck my Inspector Popatkar goes on leave, and then you are welcome to his office. But it would be quite unfair to make him move out today. He is up to his ears in clearing up. I insist always, you know, that no one goes on leave till he can show me a clear desk.'

'Very good,' Ghote said. 'But a question of office accommodation need not stop me getting down to work. Are all your cells full?'

'Cells? Cells?'

For a moment it sounded as if the superintendent had not the least idea what a cell was. Then enlightenment broke.

'But, my dear Inspector, you cannot work in a cell.'

'Why not?' Ghote asked. 'Are they in dirty condition?'

'Certainly not.'

The superintendent was shocked.

'My dear Inspector, you could eat a meal off the floor in any cell in this building with prisoners in it or not, I promise you that.'

'Then shall we go and select one as office for me?' Ghote said. 'And perhaps you could see that a stronger than regulation electric light bulb is found for it. I expect I shall be working all night.'

'All night?' the superintendent echoed hollowly. 'My dear fellow . . . '

He took off his cap and clutched hard at it with both hands as if he badly needed the reassurance of knowing that it existed in a world gone suddenly somewhat mad.

Ghote did not in fact spend all the rest of that day and the night that followed at work on the pile of papers that, item by item, had been brought to the cell – an isolated one used for solitary confinement which the superintendent had found for him. The superintendent, once he had been put on the right path, was certainly unflagging and his searching constables brought in not only the Case Diary and the copy of the First Information Report, but in addition countless curling and crumpled official forms that had been issued in connection with the fifteen-year-old case and dozens of dog-eared copies of the lengthy depositions that had been taken from various possible witnesses like the servants at Vinayak Savarkar's former home. Then there were such things as the report of the town's pathologist on the steps that had been taken with the body of the deceased and the voluminous, and ill-ordered, records of the Coroner's Committee that had deliberated the matter from its origins to a final permission for the body to be burned 'according to Hindu rites'.

So Ghote had spent hours pondering the significance of such things as the quantity of lime pickle eaten by the dead woman shortly before her demise, and what weight to put on a remark doubtfully alleged to have been made to Vinayak Savarkar by his now long since dead father-in-law, the former Municipal Chairman, regretting that he was already married and could not become his heir. Or there was the matter of why Vinayak Savarkar had suddenly visited Bombay shortly before his wife had been taken so unexpectedly ill. These and a hundred and one other things preoccupied him.

But by about three a.m. that night, after having had only two short breaks for meals, he had been so gummy-eyed with tiredness that he had simply lain down flat on the bare wooden bench that ran along one wall of the cell and had slept.

He would have abandoned his task earlier, in fact, had it not been for the workings of his conscience. Because it had not been only his determination to outwit the Municipal Chairman by the sheer violence of his attack that had provoked his announcement that he was not going to sleep until he had read through every sheet of paper that the case had given rise to. There had also been the fact that he was most unwilling to spend the night in the place where he had been instructed to find a bed.

The Eminent Figure who had so coldly given him his orders over the telephone in Bombay had, besides arranging that by way of disguise he would be a walking advertisement for a family concern, also told him what arrangements he ought to make for his stay in the town.

'You must take a bed in the retiring-room at the station,' that naggingly clear voice had said.

Unthinkingly Ghote had objected.

'But, sir, it is forbidden for people who are not bona fide travellers on the railway system to make use of such places.'

'It is an excellent retiring-room,' the voice had continued as if he himself had never spoken. 'You will be extremely comfortable there, and your expenses will not be a great charge on public funds.'

'But – '

'I myself spent several nights there when I was in the area during the election campaign. I can thoroughly recommend it.'

'Very well, sir.'

Ghote had known he ought to have refused. If a police officer was not going to obey the rules, who else would? He felt he ought to have risked the violent denunciation from the Eminent Figure that a stand on this issue might provoke.

And he had shirked it. He had allowed the comforting little thought that he could always find a hotel room for himself when he got to the town to act as a sop to his conscience.

'There will be another advantage also,' the clear voice had added. 'I shall know where to find you if I have to get in touch during the night hours.'

'Yes, sir.'

But here at the police-station the chance of putting off the actual illegal act anyhow for one night had seemed too good to miss. And now overwhelming tiredness after the hard day's work and the poor night's rest in the train had taken their toll and Ghote had slept flat on his back on the prisoner's bench.

He had however been awakened after less than a couple of hours by a particularly violent shower beating down on the tin roof of a small lean-to shed in the yard just outside the little open barred window of the cell. And after a refreshing sluice-down with a bucket of water he had set to work again.

By seven o'clock he had mastered the bulk of material the affair had generated. It had seemed at times that the now deceased District Superintendent of Police fifteen long years before had made up his mind to compensate for an evident determination not to get anywhere with the matter by the quantity of paper he had caused to be amassed. But his very protective industry had undone him: out of it Ghote was certain that he had now obtained at least two lines that even after this lapse of time ought to yield results.

He decided that the moment had come, early in the day though it was, to make a telephone call to Bombay. The Eminent Figure had been most insistent on being kept in touch with every development. Now there was something to tell him.

After some thought about where it would be safest to make this tricky call from he fixed on Inspector's Popatkar's now meticulously cleared-up office. Since in all probability every call from the town to Bombay would be monitored by some hireling of the Municipal Chairman's in the telephone exchange, he reasoned, it did not greatly matter where he set himself up and in the inspector's little room he could at least have privacy.

So sitting on the inspector's hard wooden armchair and confronting a large wall chart headed 'Pickpocketing Offences', he asked for the number of the Eminent Figure's private residence.

It took a long time for the connection to be made. Ghote registered that this could be because someone at the exchange was alerting somebody else who had been detailed to listen in on the call, or it could be only the customary delay all calls were subject to.

But at last the number was answered, and almost as soon as Ghote had said guardedly to the servant who had taken the call that 'a person' speaking from his present whereabouts wished to talk with his master the familiar over-precise voice was in his ear once more.

'This is a very early call, Inspec – '

Ghote interrupted brutally.

'Excuse me, sir, but I consider no names ought to be employed on an open line.'

'No names?' the voice said querulously.

'Sir, it is possible that someone at the exchange may be listening, and this is confidential matter.'

There came a series of crackingly loud clicks in the earpiece. Ghote briefly considered their significance, but decided that they could mean anything. Now he was able to hear the voice at the far end once again.

'. . . must impress upon you the absolute need to speak in the most general terms.'

'Yes, sir.'

'Well, have you got enough evid – Have you got that which I asked you to acquire?'

'I have some useful lines to pursue, sir.'

'Good, good. What are they?'

'I have seen a great number of documents, sir. I have been up all night studying, as a matter of fact.'

'Well, well, what is it you have learnt?'

The voice was impatient.

Ghote resumed with care.

'There is first of all, sir, one serious omission. Certain objects should have been dispatched to a certain official in Bombay. I can find no receipt from him for their arrival, although there is an official form for such transactions, and neither can I – '

'Inspector, Inspector. I cannot understand a single word of all this rigmarole. What object is this? Who should have given a receipt for them? Is this some piece of culpable negligence? Could we bring a charge – '

'Sir,' Ghote broke in, desperate protest allowing all the outrage he felt to enter uninhibitedly into his voice.

He thought like lightning.

'As regards charges, sir,' he said with deliberate slowness, 'I think that an account should be rendered in the ordinary course of business. A sum of about Rupees 20 should be in order.'

'Rupees 20? What Rupees 20 is this? Do you think I want the fellow fined a miserable Rupees 20, Inspector?'

Ghote gave up.

'It is the organs of the deceased, sir,' he said as rapidly as he could. 'They appear never to have been sent to the Chemical Examiner in Bombay. If this is so it is greatly significant, I believe. Why should they have been withheld if there was nothing to fear?'

24

'Nothing to fear, man? Of course there was something to fear.'

The outrage in the Eminent Figure's tones was only a little marred by a single loud pinging click from somewhere on the line. Ghote decided that this really was some listener being connected to the conversation. It was probably the Municipal Chairman himself.

'Are you there?' said the querulous voice.

'Yes, sir.'

'Then I repeat, Inspector, you are not trying to tell me, are you, that the fellow did not murder his wife?'

3

Ghote almost expected to hear the voice of the Municipal Chairman himself commenting sharply on this outrageously explicit statement that had just been made at the far end of the line. But no sound came.

Then the querulous voice resumed once more.

'And is this business of the missing organs the full extent of your discoveries, Inspector?'

'No, sir,' said Ghote grimly. 'There are a number of people I should like to interview also.'

'Who, man? Who?'

'I think it is better not to give names, sir.'

There was a long icy pause at the other end. During it a tiny voice could just be heard on another line talking rapidly in Marathi, a woman who seemed angry over something.

Then the Eminent Figure spoke again.

'Perhaps you are right, Mr Chaudhuri,' it said carefully.

Mr Chaudhuri? Who did the old fool think –

Then light dawned. But it was a bit late to start playing games like that now.

'Yes,' Ghote said slowly and clearly. 'I always feel, sir, that in a commercial matter of this sort the utmost discretion is necessary.'

'Yes, yes, Mr Chaudhuri. The utmost discretion.'

And the old fool, chuckling with enjoyment, rang off.

Ghote found that large drops of sweat were standing on his forehead. Outside he could see that another heavy shower had begun. He got up and went out towards the outer office. He felt the need for a large cup of coffee.

But this was something he was destined not to get.

Hardly had he entered the front office than the tall heavy figure of Superintendent Chavan came in through the outer doors wearing a uniform more dazzlingly ironed, if possible, than that of the day before.

There was an immense flurry of heel-crashing as the three constables on duty greeted him with vibrating salutes.

He acknowledged them smartly if less noisily, and then turned to Ghote.

'Good morning, my dear Inspector. I see that you have kept your promise of being up and about at this hour. I came in to see if there was anything you wanted. Inspector Popatkar's office should be at your disposal now.'

'It is indeed, sir,' Ghote answered. 'Perhaps you would care to step in there for a moment to hear how matters have gone.'

He retraced his steps to the office ahead of the superintendent, unlocked its carefully closed door on which already a card bearing his name had been inserted in the brass holder, and returned to the file-laden desk.

'Well, sir,' he said, 'certain lines of inquiry do appear to be open.'

'Good, good. What have you found?'

'First of all, sir, that the organs removed at the post-mortem do not appear to have been sent to the Chemical Examiner in Bombay. There is no report from him, and not even a returned receipt Form J stroke 804.'

The superintendent's eyes shone.

'It looks very much then, Inspector, as if there is something to suspect. And that someone also has been wilfully irresponsible. Of course, the onward transmission of the organs is not a matter for the police, as you know.'

'No, sir. It is the pathologist here that I shall have to question. One by name Hemu Adhikari.'

'No longer with us then,' the superintendent said ruefully. 'Quite a different chap up at the hospital now.'

'Yes, sir. I have already taken the liberty of asking your night sergeant who the pathologist was, and he told me that it is some years since Adhikari was here. He is understood to have taken a post in a hospital in Nagaland. But his father, a retired schoolmaster, still resides in the town. He will be one of my first visits.'

'One of your first, Inspector? You have others?'

'Yes, sir. It struck me as altogether extraordinary in view of the suddenness with which deceased died and of the nature of her fatal illness that the body was permitted to be burned and not preserved by burial. Now it is the Coroner's Committee that would grant such permission and it would not be a difficult matter, as you know, sir, for a person in a position of influence to have a say in the selection of such a committee.'

'No. No, you are right, Inspector. Quite right. Damned fine work, if I may say so.'

'Thank you, sir. And this is where I would like some help from your men. It is a matter of finding the present addresses of the five individuals listed as serving on the Coroner's Committee. I have written them out for you, sir. There is the foreman, Janardan Pendharkar, a Ram Dhulup, an individual called Bhatu – there will be a good many of them I regret – a Ram Phalke and a Govind Gokhale.'

The superintendent compressed his well-fleshed lips.

'It would not be easy, Inspector,' he said. 'None of them are uncommon names. But my men know the town inside out, I am happy to say. I will get on to it right away.'

A respectful knock came at the door.

'Come, come,' the superintendent barked out.

The door opened. It was one of the outer office constables. Under his arm he carried a newspaper, folded with geometrical neatness.

'Your paper has just arrived, Superintendent sahib,' he said. 'You gave orders it was to be brought to you at once.'

The superintendent took the paper eagerly. He turned to Ghote.

'You will excuse me one moment, my dear fellow. We are having serious flooding in the area and I need to find out what course events are expected to take.'

He began rapidly scanning the front page of the paper, uttering occasional quick grunts. Ghote had to concede that to him local flooding with all the policing problems it could bring was properly a more serious matter than a crime that had been committed fifteen years before. But he nevertheless began increasingly to boil with impatience at the superintendent's failure to issue a quick order for a search for the addresses of the members of the Coroner's Committee. The sooner they were found the sooner he could get at the Municipal Chairman where, after all, he might be vulnerable. He longed to see files and records being attacked with all the vigour in the world until the facts he wanted had been torn out of them.

'Bad, bad,' murmured the superintendent, still deeply engrossed.

He began sorting through the eight or so pages of the paper in search of some extra item inside. And then, as he found the page he wanted and flattened the puffed-up sheets on Inspector Popatkar's desk, both he and Ghote saw simultaneously a single bold heading that dominated the page.

HOLY MAN'S
FAST
AGAINST
PROBE
GOES ON

For a moment the superintendent seemed to be considering flapping the page over and pretending that nothing that concerned either of them was there. But the bold letters were too obvious. They were both staring at them, and each knew the other had seen them.

'Superintendent,' Ghote said, 'I notice there is an item there about this fast against my investigation. Is there something fresh?'

28

'Oh, no, no, no.'

'You are certain, Superintendent?'

The superintendent puffed out his fleshy lips like a man making up his mind to plunge his hands into some unsavoury substance. He put a forefinger at the top of the column and scrupulously drew it down until the very end of the story had been reached.

Then he looked up with a happier expression.

'No, it says only that he is going on,' he announced. 'This will be the sixty-first day.'

'The sixty-first,' Ghote echoed.

It had been going on longer than he realized then. That copy of *Time* magazine must have been older than he had thought.

'Yes, it is sixty-one days,' the superintendent said briskly. 'But as you will know, often such fasts go on for seventy days or eighty.'

Ghote drew in a deep breath.

'Superintendent,' he said. 'This is a matter I had been meaning to ask your advice upon. Please, what effect is it having in the town?'

Superintendent Chavan straightened his brilliantly polished belt.

'Inspector,' he said, 'I will be totally frank.'

'Yes?' Ghote said, feeling black lines of despair zig-zagging down into his inmost being.

'It is bad, Inspector. It is undoubtedly bad. The Swami in question is an important figure in the town. He established himself in a disused temple down by the river more than two years ago, and he has gained very great influence over the people.'

'He has taken up public matters before?' Ghote asked, throwing in whatever came to hand in the hope it might stave off the knowledge that this obstacle to his mission was as overwhelming as it now seemed to be.

'Oh, indeed, yes,' the superintendent answered remorselessly. 'This time last year when the monsoon had partially failed and the grain merchants were already beginning to put up their prices he went on a fast-unto-death also.'

Ghote took in the significance of that 'also'. Nefarious grain merchants and over-inquisitive police inspectors were firmly bracketed together.

'And what happened with that fast?' he asked dolefully.

'The prices came down,' the superintendent replied. 'One of the merchants was attacked by a mob.'

Ghote swallowed.

'He was killed?'

'No, no,' said the superintendent.

And then, as Ghote relaxed a little, he gave him a hard look.

'But he came out of hospital last month only,' he said.

Ghote inwardly shouldered the burden.

'I had intended always to work fast,' he said. 'Now I see I shall have to work even faster.'

A glimmer of consoling thought came to him as he spoke. He gave the bright orange egg-box resting on a corner of Inspector Popatkar's desk a little tap.

'At least I have this as a disguise,' he said. 'Luckily when I encountered the Chairman outside the station here he did not catch a glimpse of it.'

'You have spoken with the Chairman already?' the superintendent asked in some surprise.

'Yes,' said Ghote tersely. 'And now, if you please, can arrangements be made to find those addresses with the utmost dispatch?'

'Of course. Of course.'

Ghote did more than arrange for a search for the present whereabouts of the five members of that Coroner's Committee he felt might well provide him with a lead into his warmed-up case. He also asked the superintendent to get one of his men to hire him a bicycle, and he found out that there was, as he had hoped there might be, a back way out of the police-station.

If he was going to succeed in carrying on his investigation in the town with this Swami radiating opposition to him from the riverside temple, then it was plainly vital that he should be able to go about unknown until he wished to reveal himself to anybody he wanted to question.

Yet, as he left to visit the pathologist's old father, following a constable across the spacious compound of the police-station to a narrow and rusted iron gate in the high back wall, he could not help wishing that his disguise had taken some other form than the commercial vulgarity of the vibrantly orange box with its jarring blue letters.

He waited while the constable pushed and wriggled a heavy key into the lock on the barred gate and, with some hideous squeals from the rusty mechanism, succeeded in unlocking it. The man held the gate wide for him and he went through.

In the narrow, muddy and appallingly stench-ridden lane outside another constable stood. He was holding, in a very military manner, a bicycle.

It was not the machine Ghote had envisaged when he had made his request for one. He had conceived of himself astride a speedy roadster, darting like a fury here and there about the town snatching up the nuggets of information he needed. The machine the constable held must have dated from well before the Chairman's first wife had died and it looked it, every inch.

It was of immensely sturdy construction. Its handlebars were curved high and faced the world ahead with all the squareness of a battleship. Its saddle was broad, it seemed, as a bench, its leather polished by generations of well-breached British sahibs of the past, for undoubtedly this machine had belonged to them in days gone by. It had a thin but still tough canvas hood on the rear wheel to protect the legs of its ever-respectable owners from the mud and dirt of life. A neat little leather tool-bag dangled from the back of the saddle and under this there was a wide metal carrier complete with thin holding-straps.

Ghote approached, and while the constable still held the machine entirely upright, he fastened the garish egg-box on to this substantial platform. It looked as out of place there as a film-poster on a bank. But at least it was an inescapable announcement that here was anybody but the hated Inspector Ghote.

Taking the handlebars from the constable, Ghote threw his leg across the bicycle's broad saddle and settled himself comfortably. He put a foot on one of the thick rubber-blocked pedals. He pushed.

Nothing happened.

In the slimy mud of the malodorous lane the heavy back-wheel of the machine simply turned slowly round without imparting any forward motion whatsoever.

And this was darting off to snatch information out of the reluctant mass of the town.

'Push,' Ghote yelled at the two watching constables. 'Push, push, push.'

When at last Ghote had brought his well-constructed steed to the house where Hemu Adhikari, former pathologist at the town's hospital, had once lived he found it was distinguished by the possession of a particularly long frontage from the equally modest establishments of its neighbours. It lay in a district near the edge of the town occupied largely by minor professional men and the owners of small businesses – schoolmasters, lower rank civil servants, the keepers of the larger shops, Dr R. Rao, proprietor of the Rao Dispensary next to the police-station, among them. All this Ghote had learnt from the night sergeant, whose encyclopedic knowledge had confirmed in advance Superintendent Chavan's claim that his men knew their area inside-out.

Now Ghote rested his battleship-heavy bicycle against a convenient wall a fair distance from the Adhikari house and fastened it up securely with a substantial padlock which the constable who had hired it for him had said he would find, with two tyre-levers, in the tool-bag.

He stepped back and gave the machine a final survey.

Yes, it would not connect him, once he had walked away from it, with the Inspector Ghote he intended to announce himself as to the pathologist's father.

He walked down to the house and knocked briskly at the narrow door at one end of its long blank outer wall.

No one answered, and after an interval he knocked again more loudly.

A patch of blue had appeared in the solid leaden sky that had hung over the town ever since his arrival and the sun was shining. Heavy steam began rising from everything in sight. It drifted up from the thatched roofs, from the puddle-splotched lane and the gurgling drain running along its length. It mounted from the tops of the trees that could be seen rising from inside the courtyards of the houses. It even came up from the back of a donkey, which stood energetically chewing at a piece of newspaper at the end of the lane, and equally from the hunched shoulders of a wreck of a beggar propped against the far corner of Mr Adhikari's house, soundly sleeping in the confident knowledge that in this quiet district no one was going to require his professional attentions.

But the sunshine, though at once making it unpleasantly hot to be standing in the glare, did at least make the outlook more cheerful. And Ghote reflected with pleasure that his departure from the rear of the police-station had not been observed at all and that he had succeeded in pushing his sturdy machine a good way through the town, a diligent salesman for chicken-feed, without causing the least outcry.

Then the door behind him opened abruptly and he turned to see a very small old man – he could not have been an inch more than five feet – standing there looking at him. He was wearing only a white dhoti, its folds falling with severe neatness from an extremely thin waist. But in spite of the scantiness of his attire and of his lack of stature he was a figure of unshakable dignity, his back kept ramrod upright and a pair of gold-rimmed pince-nez set on his nose straight as the horizon.

In one second, it seemed, he had summed up his visitor.

'If,' he said sternly, 'you have come to sell, it would be only fair to let you know I have no intention to buy.'

4

For one nasty moment Ghote saw all his ingenious plans for slipping out of the appearance of a chicken-feed salesman and into that of a police inspector and vice-versa crumbling to nothing. He had been spotted at a glance.

Then he realized, with a disproportionate feeling of relief that brought the sweat up all over his body, that the little old upright gentleman in front of him had done no more than to suppose any caller in anonymous white shirt and trousers must be some sort of salesman.

'No, no,' he explained quickly. 'I am a police officer. My name is Ghote, Inspector Ghote. Am I correct in thinking I am speaking to Mr Adhikari senior?'

'You are speaking to Mr Adhikari. There is no Mr Adhikari junior.'

Ghote could not keep the surprise quite off his face.

'But you have a son?' he asked. 'Mr Hemu Adhikari?'

The old man's straight mouth, which had not in any case shown anything of a smile, became a degree sterner.

'I had a son,' he said. 'He no longer exists.'

Ghote experienced the faint thud of disappointment which always came to him was a trail petered out.

'He died then in Nagaland?' he inquired, unwilling to let the thread tail quite away.

An expression of sharp annoyance planted itself on the old gentleman's face.

'What is it about my son that is suddenly so important today?' he demanded. 'First one and then the other, they come knocking at my door. Is your son here? Where is your son now? I tell you my son has ceased to exist.'

Ghote put out some muttered apologies and retreated. He had learnt more than he had bargained for. Although he had been out on his trail early, someone else had been even earlier. Doubtless someone sent by the Municipal Chairman to make perfectly sure that the former town pathologist was still well out of the way.

Well, he was as far out of the way as could be, it seemed.

'Most sorry for disturbing you,' he called out one last time.

The old schoolmaster gave a general glare round the street, concentrated its last furies on the huddled form of the beggar against his house wall, as if the sight of such heaped degradation was especially displeasing to his ramrod self, and then retreated stumpily inside.

Above, the leaden sky had closed sullenly together again and

Ghote, rejoining his egg-box and bicycle, felt the first stirrings of what was doubtless to be another downpour. He mounted and began heaving round the heavy pedals of the machine with all his might.

But one flickering tongue of comfort did leap out of the ashes of his disappointment. If the Chairman had been so concerned to make sure Hemu Adhikari was still in Nagaland, then Hemu Adhikari must indeed have known something to the Chairman's discredit. And despite every move that was being made it might yet be possible to learn what that something was.

Ghote brought the machine under him to a slithering halt in the muddy street, tugged out the notebook in which he had jotted down information the night sergeant had given him, found exactly where the town hospital lay and, bodily tugging round the battleship bicycle and aiming it in a new direction, set off again at a doubly determined rate.

Dr Dahabhai Patil, the Medical Superintendent at the hospital, kept Ghote waiting for almost an hour before giving him the interview he had requested in a carefully sealed note written after he had heaved the heavy bicycle into a rack at the hospital and had thus shed once again his salesman disguise.

During all the waiting time he sat on a slatted wooden bench in the anteroom which he shared for short periods with no fewer than five other visitors to the Medical Superintendent, each bearing odd similarities of appearance in the shape of heavy horn-rim spectacles and much-flourished briefcases – Ghote decided eventually that they must be the representatives of drug firms.

Perhaps, he thought, this was the day and the hour in all the month that Dr Patil set aside for such visits. But, even if they did provide a reason for his own long wait, it was still true that in the intervals of negotiation over drug supplies Dr Patil would have had plenty of time to take advice from his near acquaintance, no doubt, the Municipal Chairman.

So by the time a peon at last came in and, salaaming perfunctorily, led him away to the Medical Superintendent he was full to the brim with seething black suspicions.

He found Dr Patil an impressive enough figure behind his large glass-topped desk. He was tall, balding, with lightly curling hair touched with silvery grey above a blandly smooth large oval face broken by a sharp nose. In spite of the oppressively damp heat he wore a tie with his white shirt. His appearance, coupled with his name and the accent in which Ghote heard him speak a few words, marked him not as a native of the place but as a Gujarati.

Ghote, confronted with this fairly formidable figure, took a quick decision. He launched into Gujarati himself, although only moderately fluent in the language.

In this part of India, unlike Bombay, gujaratis were few and far between. Would this appeal to the man's home roots establish between them a sort of link to counter any loyalty he had for the Municipal Chairman?

Dr Patil at least replied in Gujarati and seemed to be deriving some pleasure from the use of his home tongue as in answer to Ghote's polite inquiry he said he came originally from Walkeshwar, the Gujarati area of Bombay. But in what way, he asked with detectable friendliness, could he assist Inspector Ghote?

'No doubt,' Ghote said, 'you will know.'

Dr Patil made a widespreading gesture with his well-manicured left hand as much as to say. 'We all have unpleasant things to do in this life.'

'Then let me tell you,' Ghote went on cautiously, 'that in the course of my inquiries to date I have been unable to trace any reports concerning the organs of the deceased after they were removed from the body by the pathologist at this hospital.'

Dr Patil raised a hand to request a halt.

'Let me think,' he said, 'I can remember the name of the person in question.'

He lifted his eyes for a moment or two to the steadily whirring ceiling-fan just above him.

'Oh, yes,' he said, 'Adhikari. Hemu, if I am not mistaken, Adhikari.'

'That is the man,' Ghote acknowledged. 'You had him on your staff for some time then?'

Dr Patil nodded a brief negative.

'No,' he replied. 'As a matter of fact Mr Adhikari took up a post in some distant part – was it Nagaland? I think it was – shortly before my own appointment here.'

'But his name seems very familiar to you?' Ghote said.

Dr Patil smiled somewhat ruefully.

'I remember the name,' he said, 'because I seemed plagued by it in the first months of my stay here. To begin with, he left rather suddenly and we had to manage for some time without a replacement. And secondly there was the matter to which you have referred.'

'The organs of the deceased?' Ghote asked with a dart of hope.

'The organs of the deceased. I was asked what had become of them, and I had to spend a considerable amount of time making inquiries when I had many other matters I would have wished to have devoted myself to. The administration of the hospital was not all that I could have desired in those days.'

Dr Patil looked down at the glass top of his desk in mild and distant disapproval.

'And your inquiries?' Ghote asked. 'What was the result of them?'

'Negative. Totally negative. I will say for Adhikari that he was an admirably methodical fellow. He kept the most complete records. The arrival of the cadaver was duly noted. Its return under the instructions of the Coroner's Committee was equally noted. Nothing whatsoever was noted about the organs.'

'And did you make inquiries of Adhikari himself?' Ghote asked. 'You must have had a forwarding address.'

Dr Patil once more sought guidance from the whirring fan blades above him. And found it.

'Yes, I remember writing a number of letters,' he said. 'It was one of the minor irritations of my first days here.'

Suddenly he smiled.

'And,' he added, his eyes twinkling, 'I think I can tell you exactly what happened to Adhikari's replies to me.'

Ghote felt a distinct surge of hope, which even the unaccountable frivolity of the Medical Superintendent's approach to the question could not dispel.

'Yes?' he asked anxiously.

Dr Patil smiled again, benignly.

'I have no doubt,' he said, 'that Adhikari penned any number of replies to my inquiries. And that he never posted one of them.'

Ghote could only look astonished.

'Yes,' Dr Patil said, still enjoying his joke, 'that was a distinctive characteristic of Mr Hemu Adhikari's. He was perhaps the greatest writer of unsent letters this town has ever known.'

'But you came here only after he had gone?' Ghote said.

'Yes. And what did he leave me with? A considerable file of correspondence addressed to a number of surgical instrument makers, generally detailing complaints, and all of it requiring answers. And never an answer came.'

Dr Patil rubbed his large strong-fingered hands together.

'Yes,' he said. 'Since I had no pathologist I undertook to deal with the matter myself. And do you know what I discovered? That not a single one of those letters was recorded in the post-book going out.'

Ghote began to feel again that a promising trail was rapidly being lost this time in a wild undergrowth of inefficiency. But he persisted with his questions.

'You say there was no record of the organs having been dispatched to the Chemical Examiner in Bombay,' he said, 'but did you carry out any search for them here?'

'Oh, indeed, I did,' Dr Patil replied with gusto. 'In hours which I could ill spare. Down on my hands and knees myself in dusty forgotten corners of the pathology store-rooms. I told you Adhikari was methodical. Innumerable specimens were preserved there – I dare say they still are – and all meticulously labelled. But none of them was labelled as being organs removed from the body of the first Mrs Savarkar.'

The words fell like successive hammer strokes on Ghote's hopes. Taken whatever way he might, they seemed to spell the end of this particular line of inquiry. If the link he had established with Dr Patil by means of his makeshift Gujarati meant anything, then he had been told the truth and the organs extracted from the late Mrs Savarkar, with all their possibilities for analysis, had long ago been destroyed. And even if Dr Patil had all along acted in the Municipal Chairman's interests, had he ever found the stored organs he would have handed them to his friend for destruction.

Ghote rose to his feet.

There remained for him now only the hope that back at the police-station Superintendent Chavan's men had been able to discover the present whereabouts of the members of the Coroner's Committee who had deliberated over the body of the first Mrs Savarkar.

He bicycled away from the hospital a great deal more slowly than he had bicycled towards it.

Toilingly he began pushing his heavy machine through the sticky slush towards the town's main street, keeping more than half his attention fixed on the ground immediately ahead of him to avoid the lake-like puddles that dotted the mud-churned road, one of which had already sent the bicycle skewing sideways under him. The rest of his thoughts still battered at the problem of just how he was to get proof of this fifteen-year-old crime, as if by mere thinking he could force open other avenues in the dead, impenetrable mass that seemed to confront him. And a small section of his mind, too, was insistently registering the fact that he was extremely hungry and that the midday meal time had come.

As he entered the top end of the broad main street all these thoughts seemed to coalesce into a single rhythm.

'Ghote go. Go Ghote.'

'Ghote go. Go Ghote.'

With a start he realized what the words he was inwardly chanting meant. Was this some subconscious cowardice making itself heard?

It was not.

Abruptly he saw that the rhythm was nothing emanating from his own head at all. It came from a substantial crowd of citizens some fifty yards ahead of him in the middle of the wide street. They were marching in his direction in procession and were chanting the words as they marched. They even carried a banner on two swaying bamboo poles. It drooped too much in the middle to be completely legible, but the last two letters were G O and the first G H.

Icy panic gripped him from throat to knees. He was possessed of a violent desire to wheel his ironclad bicycle round anyhow on the slippery mud and to pedal off as hard as his legs could make the machine go in any direction that would take him away from the advancing mob, with its shouting emotional faces worked upon by thoughts of the good holy man slowly starving himself to death.

But, as quickly, he saw that this would not do. If an angry crowd like this saw a newcomer to the town turn and flee before them they were very likely to decide that he must be the hated Ghote. And in any chase hereabouts bare feet would have no mean advantage over bicycle wheels on the slimy surfaces of the puddle-pocked town streets.

He forced himself not to turn. More, he forced himself to cycle slowly towards the oncoming protesters.

Only when he was almost level with the head of the procession did he permit himself to bring his machine to a halt and wait by the roadside, in as natural a manner as he could force himself to show, while the chanting mob passed by.

Allowing for the ragtag and bobtail that came at the end of the procession in the way of small boys dancing and squawking, dogs yapping and snapping and a mild madman uttering from time to time shrieks of whistle-high pitch, the whole affair took a good five minutes to unroll. Ghote stood by the roadside, giving each passer-by a long uninhibited stare, and contriving in the interests of his own safety to make sure that every single protester got a good look at the egg-box on his bicycle's rear carrier.

When at last even the mild madman had passed Ghote found that he was noticeably trembling as he slowly remounted.

Perhaps these fifty or so protesters had not been too formidable. But what if they had realized whom it was standing there, and had surrounded him? He could at this moment have been lying face down in the broad puddle that spread at his feet, battered insensible even if still alive.

One thing was clear. The time at his disposal in the town was getting hourly shorter and shorter.

5

So it was a hasty meal indeed that Ghote ate before setting out again to try the other trail he had unearthed in his all-night examination of the files that had been accumulated when the sudden death of Sarojini Savarkar had been investigated fifteen years before.

Yet he felt a shade more hopeful than he had done when he had arrived at the police-station. Superintendent Chavan's claim about the efficiency of his men had not proved illusory. A team of constable clerks working without cease had succeeded in discovering the present whereabouts of all five of the men who had served on the Coroner's Committee which had, in defiance of customary procedure, granted permission for a suspected victim of poisoning to be burned instead of being buried.

And more than this, Superintendent Chavan himself had remembered that one man in particular on that committee was very likely strongly indebted to the Municipal Chairman.

'He is the fellow by name of Ram Dhulup, my dear Inspector,' the superintendent had said, his heavy frame positively bursting with pride. 'The man is accident victim, you know, and would have been altogether reduced to beggary except that some person of wealth makes him a monthly retainer.'

The superintendent had leant across his desk at this point and had beaten an absolute tattoo of finger taps on his braided cap so delighted was he with his discovery.

'I have personally myself checked with one or two very good friends of mine in the town, and I can assure you, my dear Inspector, that man is not in receipt of any kind of State pension whatsoever.'

'That is most interesting, sir.'

'It points to one person, eh, Inspector? One person who shall be nameless, I think you would agree. Hah!'

Ghote had hurried off at this, a typed list of the addresses of his five possible leads neatly folded in the top pocket of his shirt. And it was to Ram Dhulup's home that he had cycled first.

Ram Dhulup may have been in receipt of a mysterious pension from someone or other, but it cannot have been a very large one since his house was simply one of a number of mud-walled buildings, scarcely more than huts, in a lane near the river inhabited by the town's dhobis, some of whom Ghote saw down by their steps on the riverbank holding out various washed garments in the heavy breeze that forecast a new shower, forlornly hoping to get them a little drier before the new downpour came.

Sitting outside the house on a low earthen platform only just higher than the immense puddles which almost completely covered the ground in this low-lying area, there was a handsome young woman – she would be, Ghote calculated, perhaps twenty-five – busy sifting grain.

'You are the daughter of Ram Dhulup?' Ghote inquired.

The young woman was instantly and lithely on her feet. She snatched at her somewhat gaudy sari to take its end decorously across her head, though in doing so she allowed – or contrived – to let the garment slip well down from her bosom.

And, looking modestly at her feet, she giggled.

Ghote, who had seen any amount of this sort of thing in Bombay, stood waiting for an answer with what patience he could muster.

At last it came.

'Not daughter. It is wife I am.'

Ghote acknowledged his surprise. If Ram Dhulup had been a senior enough citizen to look well on a Coroner's Committee fifteen years before he ought not to have a wife of this age. However the discrepancy in years between the couple did not seem to be his immediate concern.

'Your husband is inside?' he asked.

Again the buxom young woman standing statuesquely in front of him giggled.

Again Ghote waited.

'No,' she replied at last. 'No, he is not inside.'

'He is talking with neighbours?' Ghote asked.

'No, he is not talking with neighbours.'

The sari had slipped back off the head now, and Ghote was able to see quite clearly that the young woman was, if not a beauty, decidedly attractive. And, plainly too, she knew it. The jewel in her nostril was a large one, and the hand that soon came up to carry out more play with the folds of the sari over the bosom was heavy with bangles.

Ghote took a breath and patiently went on with his interrogation.

'He has gone to buy something?'

'No, he has not gone to buy anything.'

'He is visiting friends?'

'No, it is not friends that he is visiting.'

'Ah, but he is visiting somewhere in the town?'

'No, he is not in the town.'

'Not in the town? Then where is he?'

'To Nagpur he has gone. More than three hours ago he has departed.'

'Why has he gone to Nagpur?'

She smiled at him brazenly, as much as to say 'What a ridiculously stupid question.'

'He has gone to wedding of cousin. Many guests they are having.'

'And you have not gone also?' Ghote asked sharply.

Ram Dhulup's young wife modestly looked down at the ground once again. She turned her hip outwards voluptuously to do so.

'The cousins are not knowing we are married,' she said. 'He is widower, my husband.'

Ghote thought he grasped the situation. A poverty-stricken dhobi is involved in some sort of serious accident which prevents him crouching on a stone step by the river's edge and beating lustily at other people's dirty clothes. At some point he is able to do a certain wealthy individual a much needed good turn. He finds himself afterwards with a pension, not much but enough to put him in a state of comparative affluence among his neighbours. An astute mother with a hard-to-hold daughter to get off her hands seizes on this suddenly well-off widower and before he knows what has happened to him he is married again and to a prime young wife. Some people have to know about it, but cousins in distant Nagpur, thirty or forty long miles away, can safely be left in ignorance, thus avoiding the recriminations that doubtless would have followed.

'When is your husband returning from Nagpur?' Ghote demanded sternly.

'Not for many days,' replied the buxom creature in front of him.

She did not seem at all unhappy at this.

'And where do his cousins live in Nagpur?' Ghote asked.

To his considerable surprise he was rewarded for this question with not only the address of the cousins but their name and occupation as well. He made a careful note of them, said a cold good-bye to the roving-eyed Mrs Dhulup and clambered back on to his bicycle.

He had four other Coroner's Committee members to see, but if they did not prove satisfactory he could always go quickly to Nagpur and get hold of Ram Dhulup. Perhaps by doing so he would get ahead of the Municipal Chairman, and he needed to do that only once.

The next person after Ram Dhulup on the list Ghote had been given by Superintendent Chavan was the foreman of that Coroner's Committee of so long ago, Janardan Pendharkar, a minor official in the local tax office. Ghote left his dreadnought bicycle with the dozens of others in racks inside the office compound and entered the building all ready to be the inspector from Bombay once again.

After obtaining a good many contradictory answers from the various file-carrying peons whom he had made inquiries of, he at last located the office of the ex-foreman of the Coroner's Committee.

Somewhat to his surprise he was immediately admitted when, in accordance with the system he had developed, he sent in his name in a sealed note by the peon he found lightly dozing on a bench in the corridor.

Janardan Pendharkar was a man of about sixty, round, chubby and immovable, like a little god.

'Sit, sit, Inspector,' he said with a gracious gesture but without actually giving this one client among many anything in the nature of a direct look.

Ghote would have sat immediately, only it seemed that Mr Pendharkar had not ascertained whether there was anything available to sit on, each of the three chairs in the office being heaped high with a pile of dog-eared and battered files. At last Ghote boldly took hold of the smallest stack and deposited it on the floor.

Rotund little Mr Pendharkar carefully read a document picked from his crowded desk while this was going on and only when Ghote was well seated did he give him one quick glance before fixing his eyes on his own plumply folded hands and launching into an observation.

'Please not to think,' he said, 'that I am not very well acquainted with the purpose of your visit on this occasion.'

Ghote, who now had leisure to look at Mr Pendharkar's desk more closely, saw on it a copy of a newspaper folded so that a familiar headline was uppermost. 'Holy Man's Fast Against Probe Goes On.' Mr Pendharkar was no doubt well acquainted indeed with the purpose of his visit, but with a venerated holy man fasting to death it was going to be most unlikely that he would be giving any assistance.

And at once his worst forebodings were justified.

He had opened his mouth to explain the imperative need to establish the truth of any allegations that might have been made when Mr Pendharkar addressed a further observation to his folded hands.

'Yes, Inspector,' he said, 'I know well what you are here for, and straightaway I must tell you something which I fear you ought to have known for yourself already.'

'Yes?' Ghote managed to interject.

'It is simply this. That my sole connection with the unfortunate business that has brought you here was to act as foreman of the duly appointed Coroner's Committee that investigated the matter when it occurred. And, of course, I cannot as a duly appointed officer divulge one word of the deliberations of the said committee.'

Mr Pendharkar smiled with content.

Ghote, who knew when he was beaten, apologized hastily for having troubled the gentleman and took his leave. He omitted to replace the bundle of files on the chair he had sat on.

Outside, standing among the racked bicycles of the tax clerks, he considered the situation. Thanks to the so much venerated holy man having taken his stand, and he wished he knew why he should have done so, it was plain that there was going to be little help got from anybody in the town. And if already there had been one protest march in the streets, how long was it going to be before there were more? Or before there were crowds milling about everywhere determined to expel, if not outright kill, this interloper who was forcing to his death their dispenser of wisdom?

Was it even worth attempting now to go through the rest of the list of Coroner's Committee members? Yet, if he were to do nothing, there would soon be an awkward accounting to have with an Eminent Figure back in Bombay. He would be expecting another report by telephone before long.

Wearily Ghote took out the list to see who was next on it. It was the committee member called Ram Phalke, a barber.

Then an idea flashed into his mind. He would switch round and tackle instead the man called Bhatu, a basketmaker. The basketmakers lived on the other side of the town, but he would go out of his way to go there. It was possible, just possible, that someone as cut off from the mainstream of local affairs as this Bhatu would be as a low caste citizen in a town like this, might have heard next to nothing of the agitation. If so, perhaps something could yet be got out of him about what had gone on at that Coroner's Committee all those years ago.

Lugging the ton-weight bicycle out of the rack, Ghote set off at a great rate, swerving wildly from the edge of one lake-like puddle to the edge of the next.

Ploughing along the wide main street as yet another solid shower began to fall, he saw the banner that had been carried in the morning's procession. It had been propped against the wall of the post office so that people going there had to walk right under to get in. The words on it now could be clearly read. GHOTE GO. He hunched himself yet more determinedly over his handlebars.

6

Ghote had to go through a long process of inquiry before, two-thirds of the way along the winding basketmakers' lane, a house was pointed out to him as belonging to his quarry. It was in fact the second hut sheltering a Bhatu that he had discovered, but as the first Bhatu had proved to be a boy of fourteen only, Ghote had not been faced with deciding which of them was the man he was seeking. Because, he had calculated, it was perfectly likely that the man would deny altogether that he was the person the hated Bombay inspector wanted to see.

But at last, with his clothes that had got thoroughly soaked by two successive downpours that afternoon clinging uncomfortably to his body, he was able to put his first question to the man sitting cross-legged in the doorway of the hut busily twining together thin dried rushes.

'Are you named Bhatu?'

A wide grin appeared on the man's face as he looked up.

'Oh, yes, sahib,' he said, his fingers not ceasing from their dexterous work. 'Oh, yes, I am Bhatu.'

Ghote, despite the aura of cheerful helplessness that radiated from his quarry, could not bring himself to sound less stern yet.

'Did you,' he demanded, 'serve on a Coroner's Committee that inquired into the death fifteen years ago of one Sarojini Savarkar?'

Again there came a split-mouth grin and vigorous head-shakings of agreement.

'Yes, yes, that is what I did, sahib. Never am I forgetting that time. Never, never.'

Ghote felt an actual prickle of excitement run up his back under his clinging shirt.

'You remember it well, do you?' he said. 'Then perhaps you can tell me about it.'

Bhatu's fingers did not cease to tug and twist at his pliant strips of rush, but he nevertheless leant back against the doorway of the hut in an attitude of relaxed story-telling.

'Oh, sahib,' he said, 'those were terrible days.'

'Terrible?' Ghote asked. 'How were they terrible?'

'Sahib, sahib, such a worry I was in I did not know what I was to think, which way I was to turn. Oh, sahib, you cannot expect me to forget those days.'

'I do not,' Ghote answered joyously. 'Tell me, though, just why was it that you were in a worry?'

'So many things they were telling me, sahib. And, sahib, I am a simple man. I do not know why I was taken to be on that Committee. Sahib, I had done nothing. Only baskets have I made, sahib, since I was old enough to twist a rush. And then came the police-wallas and said I must be on Coroner's Committee.'

Ghote thought he could see why poor Bhatu had been chosen for this particular committee. If you were looking for a thoroughly simple man who would not in the least understand what was going on, then Bhatu filled the bill to a nicety.

He sat himself down comfortably beside the basketmaker, reflecting that being able to make such a gesture of friendly interest was one advantage he possessed in a caste-ridden place like this.

'You were asked to tell why the late Sarojini Savarkar had died?' he said.

'Yes, yes, that is it. That is it indeed, sahib.'

'And did you learn many things about the way she had died?'

Bhatu smiled even more brilliantly than before.

'That was the trouble indeed, sahib,' he said. 'They told all the pains she had had. First the sicknesses never stopping and the great thirstiness and in the throat a burning, then the pains in the stomach and the fast coming of motions of the bowels of very bad odours, and then the pains like cramp in the lower legs and very strong and at the end the great weakness, while all along the eyes are open and there is knowing what is happening.'

Ghote listened in considerable astonishment. It was fifteen years, after all, since Bhatu had heard these symptoms described, and yet here he was retailing them all as if they had happened to someone he had seen only that week. But what was even more astonishing was that here were being retailed one by one the symptoms of acute arsenical poisoning, just as he himself had read them in Gross's *Criminal Investigation* amid the hurried preparations for his departure from Bombay.

'You have told much,' he said cautiously to Bhatu.

'Oh yes,' replied the basketmaker cheerfully. 'I remember much. Many times have I thought about those terrible days.'

'Those terrible days of the Coroner's Committee?'

'What else?' Bhatu said in surprise. 'No other terrible days have I known.'

'But why were those days so terrible?' Ghote asked.

'Because of what they told, the others,' Bhatu answered. 'So strongly they told. These are what happens when bad food is by mistaken eaten they said. And I knew it was not so.'

'You knew it was not so?'

'But do you not know,' Bhatu asked, his fingers actually ceasing to move for a few moments, 'do you not know the way my mother's cousin's aunt is dying long ago?'

'No,' said Ghote.

'In great agony she is dying,' Bhatu said. 'First there is the sickness, and the terrible thirstiness and feeling of burning in the throat, and then the pains in the stomach, then the many motions and the great smell, then the pains of cramp in the lower legs and afterwards the end with all the while the eyes open and knowing.'

'Your mother's aunt's cousin died like that?' Ghote asked.

'No,' said Bhatu.

Ghote's hopes crumbled to nothing in an instant.

'No,' Bhatu repeated firmly. 'Not my mother's aunt's cousin. It was my mother's cousin's aunt. And I knew it well that she died because, being nearly blind, she took instead of a sweet-meat at a wedding feast an amount of rat poison that had been left there also.'

Rat poison, Ghote thought. At the time of Bhatu's mother's cousin's aunt arsenic had been very generally employed as a rat poison.

'So you see,' Bhatu went on, his whole face expressing de-lighted joy at being able to tell Ghote what he wanted to hear, 'all the time in those terrible days I am knowing that they ought to be thinking that the memsahib was dying of poison. But no one is saying.'

He stopped and gave Ghote one single almighty grin.

'In the end,' he avowed, 'I am telling them. I, Bhatu the basketmaker, am telling.'

He sighed like a pair of bellows.

'But they are very steady not to listen,' he said.

No wonder, Ghote thought. He pictured the scene to himself. This simple fellow, brought in to make up the quota for the Coroner's Committee in the certainty that he would not in any way see through the deceit that was to be practised, and it turning out that his mother's aunt's cousin – no, cousin's aunt – had died in precisely the same way that the late Mrs Savarkar had done. No wonder they had ignored the poor fellow into silence.

And now he was going on with his long-remembered tale of woe.

'So you can see,' he said, 'often I am wondering what did happen in those terrible days. Why was I wrong? Because you know in the end they brought in Verdict.'

'Yes,' said Ghote, 'a verdict of Death by Misadventure.'

'You are knowing that?' Bhatu said, his eyes lighting up. 'And you are knowing what it means?'

'It means they said she had died by accident.'

'Yes,' Bhatu rejoined. 'She died by accident and all along I was wrong.'

'Wrong?' said Ghote.

'Oh yes, wrong. It was by bad food not by poison that she died.'

'But,' Ghote said carefully and slowly, 'you know that she died just in the way your mother's cousin's aunt died who ate arsenic.'

'But no,' Bhatu replied. 'That is what I am telling. But the memsahib did not die that way. She died from bad food.'

And, although Ghote spent altogether another full half-hour there outside the basketmaker's hut, he could not succeed in convincing Bhatu that what he thought he knew to be so was not so. Fifteen years before he had been told that it was not arsenic but bad food that had brought about the death of Sarojini Savarkar and so it would always be.

At last Ghote got up and took his leave, reflecting that though he had failed to obtain a witness ready to denounce the working of the Coroner's Committee he had at least acquired one thing of value – the personal certainty that the late Mrs Sarojini Savarkar had really died from arsenic poisoning.

He reflected, too, that he must get hold of Ram Dhulup. If something had been put over on the Coroner's Committee the pensioned dhobi was most likely to be the man responsible for doing it. A train journey to Nagpur was indicated at the first opportunity.

And, after all, there were too the organs that had been removed from the body. Might they still exist somewhere in the hospital store-rooms? Dr Patil had said it was possible. And they would constitute the proof of poisoning that poor Bhatu was incapable of supplying. Here was something else he would spare no pains to pursue to the end.

As he cycled slowly off through the mud he saw a man walking towards him carrying with care a folded newspaper. He was not certain but it looked very like the identical edition he had seen that afternoon on chubby Mr Pendharkar's desk.

He bent to pedal with a will. The news of the holy man's continuing fight against him was spreading to the most neglected corners of the town.

He found too that the news was certainly well in circulation in the middle of the town when he came to tackle the other two members of the Coroner's Committee, first Ram Phalke, barber, at work beneath the tattered awning that protected his raised platform pitch just off the main street, and then Govind Gokhale, letter-writer, actually sitting not ten yards from the banner that now draped the entrance to the post office.

Ram Phalke had flown into a tearing rage the moment he had understood who Ghote was. Waving, in a highly ominous manner, the open razor that a moment earlier he had been lovingly curling round a squatting customer's jawline, he yelled and shrieked that he would have nothing to do with such an impious project, that he and his family had often derived great benefits from the holy man who had deigned to grace the town with his presence and that it was a scandal that anyone should attempt to flout him.

Govind Gokhale had taken a different tack. But one no less effective. He had forgotten, he said. He had really forgotten almost that he had ever served on that particular Coroner's Committee. He had served on so many he explained, as the illiterate old farmer hunched in front of his table under the post office portico had looked on in amazement. He was a man, he had let Ghote understand, of some consequence. He had a great deal to do. Affairs pressed down on him. There were letters to be written in pencil, in pen, or typed even, if the client could afford it. He advised these poor people. They needed him. How among all this could he remember trifling circumstances fifteen years ago? Was it fifteen only? He had thought it was more.

But Ghote had not felt too discouraged. The information that he had got from happy open Bhatu – and before the holy man's campaign had awed him into silence too – was a positive gain. Ghote warmed it to his breast as if it was one of the double-sized eggs that still followed him on the bicycle carrier in their grease coating and their loudly marked cardboard box.

He made his way, with the smell of evening meals nearing readiness wafting into his nostrils on the damp air, out of the town centre along towards the railway station. It might be late in the day and he was certainly feeling tired enough after his two nights with next to no sleep. But he made up his mind he would not yet seek a bed in the station retiring-room as the Eminent Figure had so insistently advised. He would ask instead if there was still a train to Nagpur, and if there was he would damn well take it. He might not have the widespread resources of the Municipal Chairman, but at least he could move with speed.

It was the station-master himself, an elderly individual with a prominent pair of silver-rimmed spectacles with one cracked lens, out of which he viewed the whole world with a good deal of suspicion, of whom Ghote made his inquiries about whether there was still a train to Nagpur.

And from whom he received a most unexpected answer.

'Train to Nagpur?' the old man said testily. 'Of course there is no train to Nagpur, not today, not tomorrow, not the next day.'

'But surely trains must run to a place like Nagpur more often than this?' Ghote said.

'Run? Run? Of course they are running to Nagpur every two hours.'

'But you said there were none, damn it, man.'

Ghote too expressed irritation. He had been a long time with little sleep.

The station-master's spate of rage died totally away.

'Is flooding,' he explained. 'All the timetable is most thoroughly upset. The line is cut from early this morning and all the time they are ringing through, telling first this then that. How am I to run a station in these conditions?'

'Flooding?' Ghote asked in sheer amazement. 'You mean that the line to Nagpur is impassable?'

'Of course that is what I am meaning,' the station-master shouted suddenly, his rage returning as swiftly as it had gone. 'That is what I am telling you, isn't it? The line to Nagpur is cut. The road also. Any moment I am expecting to learn that the telegraph is out of action. And then where will I be getting my instructions from?'

Ghote forbore to tell the old man that if his instructions were so contrary he would be better off without any. There was something much more important to think about.

So Nagpur had been cut off from the town since early that morning. Then how had Ram Dhulup managed to go there for the wedding of his cousin? Or, not to put too fine a point upon it, where was the Municipal Chairman keeping Ram Dhulup in hiding since plainly the former dhobi had never attempted to go to Nagpur at all?

7

Ghote very nearly took his bicycle once more and pedalled straight back to the dhobi's quarter to ask Ram Dhulup's wife the answer to the question that had erupted so forcefully on his horizon with the news of the effect of the floods. But almost at once he reflected that the buxom Mrs Dhulup, after being so reluctant to tell him anything at all at first, had suddenly come out very generously with the name and address of the cousins at Nagpur. No doubt this had simply been because she knew very well that there were no such people.

A hot flush spread down his body at the thought of how nearly he had gone rushing off to Nagpur to the invented address he had been given so glibly. How the Municipal Chairman would have laughed when some hireling at the station – perhaps even the old station-master himself – had telephoned through to tell him that the intrusive Bombay CID man had safely departed on a wild-goose chase.

A wave of tiredness flooded over him in the wake of this thought. At some time he would have to tackle again that proud liar who had married Ram Dhulup. But he would need to have all his wits about him. In the meantime sleep called so insistently that it dulled all pangs of conscience and he sought out without hesitation the retiring-room of which the Eminent Figure had spoken so highly and had made such good, if illicit, use on his own visit to the town.

He found too that the Eminent Figure had spoken the exact truth. The retiring-room did great credit to the old and patchily fury-shaken station-master. It was as excellent an example of its kind as Ghote had ever seen. There was what the railways' descriptions call 'modern sanitation' as well as a couple of shower cubicles positively gleaming with cleanliness. And in the bedroom cubicles there were neatly made-up beds with clean white sheets on them, deliciously inviting.

Ghote sank his last scruples and booked himself in. The old station-master actually salaamed as he accepted the bribe.

Next morning Ghote found the tearing zeal that had been with him since he had set foot in the town appeared to have vanished almost to nothing. He told himself at first that this was merely because even a good night's sleep had not wiped out all his accumulated tiredness. Then he put this unexpected hollowness down to the effect of his near-defeat in the matter of the train to Nagpur the evening before. Next he tried to persuade himself that he was suffering from guilty feelings over having broken the regulations concerning the occupation of railway retiring-rooms.

But all along he knew secretly that his sudden reluctance to face the new day sprang from one thing only. It had come to him while he slept: he had a task that had to be performed, and the sooner the better.

He had to go and see the holy man face to face on this the sixty-second day of his fast. He had to find out from him, if he could, why he was opposing the investigation and he had to persuade him to change his mind. Only in this way could he buy himself enough time to complete his inquiries.

But he did not want to do it.

So he lingered atrociously under a luxurious shower and then went to the station restaurant where he indulged himself for breakfast with, not 'Tea in cup (Readymade 200 cc)' as the tariff called it, but with 'Tea in pot (285 cc with separate milk and sugar)'. Yet, though he also ate heartily, he could not somehow bring himself to 'Scram Bled Eggs (Eggs 3 Pieces)', reluctant to eat any of the objects which had haunted him since he had come to the town, and which he supposed he would still have to take with him wherever he went.

At last he made his way, slowly as his heavy bicycle dictated, to the police-station where he found Superintendent Chavan already seated at his desk with a substantial work-load fast disappearing in front of him. And to the superintendent he reported, as convention imposed, an outline of the events of the day before. The superintendent was sympathetic, particularly when he heard about the disappearing dhobi.

'Yes,' he said, reaching forward to stub out a cigarette and adjust the position of his cap on the desk beside the gleaming polished brass ashtray, 'yes, I am sorry to tell that this is exactly the type of action to expect from the person-in-question. He is a man of dynamic efficiency, I am telling you. That is why he has risen up so fast in the town altogether. He is not native-born here, you know, no more that I am. But I have heard a good deal about his early days in the town. They are something of a legend with us.'

Ghote let him talk on. He knew he should not really be spending time listening to what amounted to no more than gossip about the Municipal Chairman years before his first wife died. But he knew also that unless he was sitting in the super-intendent's spick-and-span office he should be out on his way to see the holy man.

'Yes,' said the superintendent, leaning his heavy bulk back-wards in his substantial desk-chair, 'yes, that man, you know, came to the town some twenty-five years ago with not an anna to his name. He had lost everything, his parents and whatever property they had had, as a result of communal strife. He was however Brahmin so at least the path to prosperity was open to him.'

He waved his right hand in the air to indicate the width of opportunity that had been open to the newly-arrived Vinayak Savarkar and that same right hand ended, as Ghote had known it would, obsessively stroking the uniform cap on the desk top.

'I do not know the details of his early days,' Superintendent Chavan went on, 'but quite soon he was in the contracting busi-ness in a small way, and year by year this became a bigger way. Other businesses in the town were driven into ruin. There was talk, I am told, about greatly adulterated cement. But nothing was ever proved. And then, quite suddenly, he was the next most powerful man in the town to the then Municipal Chairman, who had great interests in property. So the contractor putting up buildings all over the place, and the property-owner with land everywhere soon formed an alliance.'

The superintendent reluctantly removed his hand from his cap.

'Unfortunately for him,' he said, 'that alliance could not be strengthened, since he had married shortly after coming here, and there was the then Chairman with one daughter only.'

He laid a finger confidentially on the side of his somewhat fleshy nose.

'She is ugly as sin, poor woman,' he said. 'I do not like to think what that man suffered to get the little son he has now.'

He leered hard before resuming.

'But she was going to be rich as the very devil, and the father was married still to a wife who would bear him no more children. It was a terrible situation. And that is where this rumour you have doubtless heard of from your reading of the files comes in.'

Ghote duly produced what he had been asked for.

'That was this reported remark of the former Chairman's?' he asked. 'This "If only you were able to marry my daughter, my dear Vinayak"?'

'Yes, that was it,' agreed the superintendent. 'God knows whether it was ever really said. But everybody knows what happened straightaway after.'

'The terrible pains in the stomach and swift death of Mrs Sarojini Savarkar,' Ghote concluded.

The words seemed to be a noisy bell summoning him to duty. He stood up.

'Well, Superintendent,' he said, 'I must not stay here all the day talking. I must get at the whole truth of the business some-how.'

'So what are you going to do now, my dear fellow?'

Ghote drew himself together.

'I am going to visit the holy man,' he said, 'and see if I cannot get this ridiculous opposition brought to an end.'

But for all his decisiveness in front of Superintendent Chavan it was a leaden cyclist indeed who made his way out of the town to conduct his interview with the obstructive Swami. In his ears the faintly ominous directions the superintendent had given him rang still. 'He is easy to find, my dear Inspector. You have only to go out along the road beside the river and you will see. You will see.'

And it had been plain from first striking the road, with the wide-swollen river running lustily beside it, that it would not be at all difficult to find the holy man. Every few yards a small party of people was to be seen either going to obtain advice or returning with expressions of almost vacant happiness on their faces – eloquent testimony of the holy man's power.

But it seemed that the Swami had chosen to give his advice from well outside the town, and, as Ghote cycled on under the heavy grey of new rain clouds, the groups of advice-seekers at last became fewer and fewer. He was even beginning to wonder whether he had not after all mistaken the way when at last he saw the holy man.

He was unmistakable, sitting all alone beside a dangle-rooted banyan tree in the dark shade of which it was just possible to make out the short black stump of a lingam.

Hardly, thought Ghote, the ruined temple he had imagined he would find the holy man in, but come to that he had not somehow expected that the Swami would be a Jain either yet a member of that sect he undoubtedly was. This was plain to see from his voluminous pure white robes, from the little white square of cloth he wore over his mouth, designed to prevent his accidentally swallowing and destroying the least living thing, and from the soft brush that lay propped against his knees as he squatted patiently looking out across the wide brown expanse of the river, a brush whose purpose it was gently to sweep any area where its possessor was going to sit lest he crush an insect in doing so.

Some fifteen yards away, Ghote dismounted from his bicycle and laid it down by the roadside, careful not to smirch the startling orange of his protective egg-box on the machine's rear carrier. Then he approached the holy man.

A plan, of some cunning, had formed in his mind. He would begin, not by tackling the Jain directly, but by appearing to be seeking spiritual comfort in general.

He stopped in front of the squatting white-masked dreamy-looking figure and made a reverent salaam.

When the elderly priest remained quite silent Ghote eventually spoke.

'I have come for advice,' he said.

He expected that such a well-known dispenser of comfort and exhortation would begin making pertinent inquiries at this point. But the reply he got surprised him.

'There is only one thing to tell,' the Jain said. 'Do no injury to any living thing. That is the way.'

Ghote pondered this unexpected remark for some moments. It did not seem to fit in with the campaign of injury that had under this old man's auspices been mounted against himself. The procession of protesters yesterday would have done considerable injury to a living thing if they had realized that the salesman on the bicycle watching them go by was the hated Inspector Ghote.

At last the resentment he always felt at any form of spiritual domination, and which he had been keeping in check hitherto, broke out.

'To injure nothing,' he spluttered. 'That is all very well. But it is Inspector Ghote you are speaking with. The Inspector Ghote who is here because he very strongly suspects that Vinayak Savarkar may have done grievous injury to his former wife. And very well you know that this is so.'

The Jain looked up at him with a placid smile.

'My son,' he replied, 'I am knowing nothing. I am not knowing who is this Vinayak Savarkar even.'

'But – but – '

Ghote found himself totally incoherent with rage. What pious trick was this?

The Jain smiled again, a slow beautiful smile.

'My son,' he said gently, 'perhaps it is the Swami at the temple round the bend in the road that you seek.'

Ghote saw his mild eyes gently blinking up at him.

'Most people passing by go to seek that Swami,' the old man said.

The ruined temple where the proper holy man held court was very easy to find round the gentle bend in the road not a hundred yards past the spot where the Jain sat. It was an old low-roofed building set among a grove of sweeping-branched pipal trees. In front of it there was a considerable strand where the river gently looped. On this were pitched a handful of temporary huts made from palm thatch, evidently by people who had come from a distance to be present during the Swami's fast. There was nothing like a really good fast to attract onlookers, and invariably those onlookers were wholly on the side of the fasting man.

Ghote cycled on until he reached the first of the pipals. He dismounted and leant his weighty machine up against one of the gnarled and creased trunks, taking care to snap round the rear-wheel the padlock and chain and to take with him the egg-container.

You cannot trust the sort of people you would find here, he said to himself with savagely drummed-up cynicism.

He advanced to the temple steps.

The inside of the building was dark and cool. For a little while Ghote could see nothing in it but the vague outlines of two rows of short pillars running down each of the side walls until they were lost in the darkness. But as his eyes became accustomed to the gloom he was able to make out more.

There were quite a few people, it seemed, inside the low-roofed building. Not far beyond the entrance doorway, in fact, there were half a dozen beggars, squatting or stretched listlessly displaying their poverty or their sores, silent at present, waiting no doubt till he should come right by before setting up their inevitable beseeching clamour. Farther inside a number of women were moving about here and there on mysterious business. Most of them were old and bent, hunched figures in white saris, but two or three appeared younger, wearing coloured saris and carrying heavy pots on their heads. There were some men as well, Ghote observed. One of them was ringing a small handbell at intervals, its tinkle deadened by the massive stone walls. Another, a man wearing a white dhoti coming well down to his ankles and a short pink vest, was carrying a large gong and striding about, an expression of blissful contentedness on his face. As Ghote watched he stopped and began to strike his gong quite softly with a knobbed stick. It gave out a low melodious note.

Somehow Ghote accepted it as a signal. He entered the

temple and, ignoring the immediate whining clamour of the beggars, moved quickly down towards the far end.

As he had expected, it was here that the holy man was installed.

Thanks to a patch of daylight that came through the roof where one of the time-blackened granite slabs had fallen in, Ghote was able to get a good view of the fiercely bearded figure sitting cross-legged in an alcove between two of the wall pillars, keeping perfectly still and hardly regarding the comings and goings.

Approaching yet nearer, Ghote saw that the Swami was sitting on a mat which covered most of the floor of the alcove. On the mat were a number of framed photographs, of other holy men to judge from their matted and ash-strewn hair. Each one was in a different frame, some of silver, others of much battered wood, most with small marigold garlands over them. The smell of the decaying flowers was sharp on the cool air. Behind the Swami, neatly rolled up, was his bedroll, dyed to the same orange colour as his robe.

But all details faded into insignificance beside the visage of the holy man. Hair positively gushed out of his head and his face at every point. It jutted forth, defying the ashes that had been liberally sprinkled on it, and it curled angrily. Inside this lively forest it was just possible to make out two deep-set baleful eyes, a thin hooked nose and two small segments of cheek. And even this small amount of flesh had about it an unmistakable look. It seemed to be not so much human skin as some vaguely luminous substance, glowing with a pale inner light.

It was the flesh of a fasting man.

For a long while Ghote stood looking. Somewhere behind him in the temple a woman began chanting those verses from the Gita in which the god, who has chosen to be Arjuna's charioteer in his fight with his uncles, explains the need to do battle. The ash-covered, sprouting-beard Swami seemed not even to hear. He remained still as a statue, and only the bright burning eyes, deep in their sockets, betrayed the fact that he was awake and alert. No one went near him, though it was perfectly obvious that all the life of the dim low-roofed building was revolving round this one still figure.

At last Ghote decided that the time had come to break through the trance-like atmosphere, shatter what it might to do so.

He took three or four brisk steps forward until he was standing at the edge of the stone platform of the alcove and confronting the holy man face to face.

'My name is Ghote,' he said. 'Ganesh Ghote, Inspector of Police, Bombay.'

He had known from the moment he set eyes on this figure that this was no occasion for guile. The direct approach and nothing else was what was needed.

For four or five long seconds the Swami remained silent and motionless. Then the lips under the jutting beard parted.

'Inspector Ghote,' said a harsh, and it seemed scornful voice.

'Yes,' Ghote replied boldly, though with the attendants hovering in the background he felt obliged to keep his voice low. 'Yes,' he repeated. 'It is I, Inspector Ghote, the man you are fasting against.'

'What have you come here for? Here?' demanded the fierce face not two feet away from his own.

Ghote drew himself up.

'I have come,' he said, 'to request that you cease this agitation against my presence in the town.'

'Request denied,' snapped the ferocious old man.

'Why?' Ghote demanded, low-voiced and urgent. 'Why? Why are you denying? Why are you supporting this man? Why are you obstructing justice?'

The Swami glared back at him, his eyes spitting.

'I tell you,' he snarled, 'that man is to be left in peace. I have said.'

'But why? Why?' Ghote asked again.

'It is enough that I have said,' the Swami answered. 'Now go. While you are here in this town I will fast. Fast to death.'

'I will not go,' Ghote said, a counter-anger coming up to boil and bubble in his veins. 'I will not go. I am here as an

62

investigating officer. I have been ordered to investigate, and investigate I will until my case is completed. What are you doing standing in the way of justice like this?'

But even this appeal to higher things fell, it seemed, on totally deaf ears.

'Go. You are not wanted. Go. Go.'

'But listen,' Ghote expostulated, 'I will find the truth, and whatever it is I will report. So if Mr Savarkar is not guilty of anything that is what I will find. What have you to fear in that?'

Again the gushingly bearded Swami was adamant.

'You are not wanted here, poking and poking into a man's life,' he said. 'And until your back is turned on this town I will be fasting. Unto death.'

The translucent skin blazed in anger.

Ghote tried changing his track.

'But what if he is guilty?' he asked. 'Is it right to shield him from the law? There must be one law for all. For the rich and for the poor.'

'And I say you are not to break the peace of that man,' the Swami grated back at him, every inch fury.

'No,' Ghote returned. 'That is wrong. I am telling you there is prima facie case. It is my duty to investigate. And it is yours as citizen before the law not to stand in my way.'

The fierily-bearded ash-smeared face glared back at him.

'I am fasting to death. To death. Or till you go.'

Ghote shook the egg-box he was carrying between his two hands in the intensity of his emotions.

'If necessary,' he said in as severe a voice as he could muster, 'I will have you charged with obstruction. I will not allow investigation to be hindered.'

'You will arrest a man fasting to death?' snarled the Swami. 'You will arrest on deathbed itself? No one has succeeded in doing that before. It would be necessary to shoot a hundred people, a thousand people, two thousand to get me from this temple.'

And abruptly the blazing eyes dropped from Ghote's face to his midriff.

'What is it you have got there?' the old man asked, with not a jot of abated sharpness.

'It is eggs, eggs only,' Ghote said.' But you must listen now – '

'Eggs? He is bringing in here eggs,' the Swami exclaimed in even louder tones.

Ghote, extremely unwilling to have his presence here among so many ill-wishers made known, shushed the old man angrily.

'Why are you objecting?' he said. 'It is only a box I happened to be carrying with me.'

'It is carried to disgust me,' the Swami retorted at a new pitch of cantankerousness. 'Well you are knowing that the egg is equally forbidden to pass the lips as any meat. And into this temple you are bringing them. Go. Go now. Go this instant. Or I will curse you.'

Again the voice was growing louder and louder. Ghote sensed various movements in the darkness of the temple behind him. He decided that there could be no purpose served in staying any longer in face of this ridiculous intransigence.

'Very well,' he said rapidly. 'I am going.'

The Swami fell silent, but he was still glaring horribly.

'I am going,' Ghote repeated. 'But I am giving this warning. If you continue to obstruct course of justice I shall have absolutely no alternative but to seek arrest warrant from nearest magistrate.'

And even as he said the words he knew that that magistrate would almost certainly be a bosom crony of the Municipal Chairman's.

But at least the cantankerous figure of the Swami was silent again. Ghote turned on his heel, and, holding the despised box of eggs stiffly out in front of him, stamped out of the hall.

8

Back in the reassuring sanity of the police-station, Ghote gave Superintendent Chavan a generalized account only of his experiences at the ruined temple.

'Ah, yes,' said the superintendent gravely, commenting on the

Swami's attitude, 'he is very bad-tempered man, but very holy also.'

Ghote accepted the judgement. After all the holy man was a factor in the life of the town, and, one thing that was absolutely clear was that the superintendent and his men did know the town and what went on in it from A to Z. And, though in general many a doubtful character lay disguised under the matted hair, ashes and orange robes of a holy man, it was also true that many a true holy man did not feel bound to express himself in gentle and sympathetic terms.

'Well,' Ghote said dolefully, 'one thing is certain: he is not going to stop his fast for me.'

'Yes, that is so,' Superintendent Chavan agreed with conviction. 'And of course also he is a man of very great age.'

'It was difficult to see in the darkness of the temple,' Ghote hazarded.

'No,' said the superintendent firmly, 'he is definitely eighty years old at the least. And he is not strong.'

'Not strong,' Ghote admitted reluctantly.

'So it is a question how long this fast-to-death will last.'

'Yes, yes. That is the question, Superintendent. You are quite right. But I suppose men of that age have fasted for as many as seventy days or more even, without any undue incident occurring.'

Ghote, faced with the fury that would beyond doubt break out in the town if the holy man were to die, had not been able to bring himself to plainer words. The superintendent was under no such restraint.

'Yes, yes,' he said with a trace of impatience, 'hale and hearty old men have fasted for perhaps as long as you have stated. But do not mistake. This individual is not at all hale and hearty. Against strict medical advice has he acted.'

'Yes,' Ghote said.

He sat in front of the superintendent's admirably orderly desk and looked down at his feet. Slowly he forced himself to brace back his shoulders.

'So I am left with only one remaining course of action,' he said. 'I must carry out personal questioning of chief suspect.'

'You are going to see the Municipal Chairman?' the Super-intendent said, his voice rising up in awe.

'I am going to see the Municipal Chairman.'

But Ghote's resolution was to be subjected to a long chill before it could be put into effect. The Municipal Chairman, telephoned from the police-station, regretted that extreme pressure of business made it impossible for him to see Inspector Ghote of the Bombay CID – until seven o'clock that evening at his home.

Ghote succeeded in filling in the afternoon profitably enough as it turned out. But the wait gave his precarious ardour a long time to cool.

He embarked on another frustrating telephone call to the Eminent Figure, patiently conveying in guarded language various requests for investigations to be made back in Bombay, such as a search in the Chemical Examiner's records for any trace of the missing organs having been received. The whole business of making the call took him more than an hour, and at the end he wondered whether the Eminent Figure really had grasped everything he wanted doing and how urgent it all was.

After this came a refresher course with the Sarojini Savarkar Case Diary in preparation for the expected battle-of-wits of the evening ahead.

But at last the time set by the Chairman drew near and Ghote, in accordance with a plan he had worked out as soon as he had realized what it was he had to do, changed into borrowed police uniform and ordered the town's most prominent taxi to call for him at the police-station.

If he was going to venture into enemy territory, especially after the warning he had received from the Chairman himself, then he wanted to invest his visit with all the panoply of officialdom he could muster. And as a last precaution he said to the superintendent just before going out to the taxi, a rust-edged old De Soto, 'If I am not back in two hours, kindly come and fetch me yourself.'

Then, ready as he ever would be, he set out.

The run to the Chairman's house on the outskirts of the

town should not have taken long, and it would have been accomplished easily inside the time Ghote had allowed for it, if the pride of the town's taxi fleet had not expired ignominiously some way from its destination.

Its engine just died away completely, and the big old car drifted to an absolute halt in the middle of the road.

The driver, a keen-looking young man with the pockets of his bush-shirt positively jammed with assorted screwdrivers and small spanners, was out of his seat in an instant.

'Aha,' he said joyfully, 'I know exactly what is wrong with her, the old bitch. Two seconds and she will be right as rain only.'

When the two seconds had lengthened into a quarter of an hour without the least sign of life from the old car's engine, Ghote, who was becoming a little anxious about his seven o'clock deadline, got out of the vehicle in his turn and suggested that it might be worth stopping a passing tonga, of which he had seen a good many taking the wealthier citizens of the town home from the day's labours.

'Not at all, not at all,' the young man said. 'This is quite small inconvenience only. By the time you have hailed tonga I will already be at Chairman's house.'

Ghote turned away and left him to his internal adjustments. But he had seen a disquieting number of engine parts lying on the running-board of the old car.

He gave the boy another five minutes, exactly. Then he marched back to him.

'It is too late now,' he announced firmly. 'I will stop the first tonga I see.'

And of course not a tonga came in sight.

Ghote fretted and fumed. He would not have put it past the Chairman to cancel the whole interview on the grounds that he was late. At the car, the driver seemed to be doing nothing but removing more pieces.

Ghote came back to him.

'Exactly how far is the house from here?' he asked.

The boy wiped his hands thoroughly on a scrap of dirty rag.

'Oh, you could not walk in the time,' he said.

Ghote looked round for some landmark. There was the bulky mounded shape of the town tank where water was stored for the time when the river was liable to run too low. But he did not know where this lay in relation to his destination.

'How far is it exactly, I am asking,' he demanded.

'It is a mile, more than a mile,' the boy answered.

Ghote looked at his watch. If he ran at a steady pace . . .

'I am going,' he announced.

'It is two miles and a half,' the boy said.

Ghote fought down a desire to lash out at him. He turned on his heel and set off at a jog-trot along the softly damp road.

He had gone less than two hundred yards when the old De Soto came coughing and spluttering up behind him. The boy was leaning out of the driver's window.

'I am telling,' he shouted. 'I know this old bitch backwards.'

'All right,' Ghote shouted back, looking up at the rain-threatening sky. 'I will take the ride.'

'Then jump in quick,' the boy answered, reaching back and letting the rear door flap open. 'It is not good idea to be stopping.'

Ghote sprinted forwards as the old car began drawing away from him. His right foot splashed gigantically in a puddle, dirtying his smart borrowed uniform trousers up to the knees. He clutched at the swaying door handle and heaved. He got a foot on the running-board. It lurched ominously under his weight. He hauled himself by main force into the car's interior.

And scarcely had he flopped back on to the seat, which he found well strewn with parts from the engine, when the car came to a brake-squealing halt, its motor mounting to a joyful roar.

'We are here,' said his driver.

Ghote got out again and appraised the building in front of him.

It was certainly impressive. A high wall of packed earth, whitewashed and barbed-wire topped, surrounded it with only an enormous pair of carved gates breaking the defences. Through them could be seen the house itself, marked out from its neighbours down the road by possessing three storeys, and a remarkable large garden dotted with flower-beds and fruit trees and all in excellent order.

Ghote looked down at his mud-spattered trousers. He had meant to confront any magnificence he might meet with all the majesty of the law. Now he was as bedraggled as any ordinary home-coming bicycling clerk this wet monsoon day.

But there was nothing for it except to call through the high carved gates to the tall turbaned chaprassi he saw strutting about beyond them. And when this lordly being had dragged open both halves of the double-gates all Ghote could do was march in with as much dignity as he could muster and go on up the well-tended gravel drive to the wide studded front door of the house itself.

At least, he found glancing at his watch, the time was exactly seven o'clock.

He rang at the doorbell. Soon the sound of bare feet slapping on marble came to him and a neatly uniformed bearer opened the door.

'Inspector Ghote, Bombay, to see Mr Savarkar.'

He said it as loudly as he could.

'Please enter, Inspector. You are expected.'

Ghote felt a dart of pleasure. At least the Chairman had reacted to his intended visit.

He followed the bearer into a chequered marble hall, and on through it down a wide corridor smelling of new paint and into a small room where he was left to wait.

After he had been there for some ten minutes he started taking stock of his surroundings. The room was furnished with what seemed to be cast-offs from other places, a stuffed sofa with a rent in the yellow material covering it, a brass tray on a wooden stand that trembled shiveringly at the least touch, a wooden almirah whose door would no longer properly close. There was only one narrow window. It looked out on to the low-growing margosa tree right up against the side of the house somewhere.

Everything seemed very quiet.

Ghote sat down cautiously on the old sofa. He crossed his

legs in such a way that the worst affected part of his trousers could dry a little.

When he next allowed himself to look at his watch he saw that it was now twenty-five past seven.

His trousers had definitely dried in patches. He went across to the door, opened it a little and peered out. Nobody was to be seen. He retreated and began rubbing at the mud splashes where they looked as if they would brush off.

When he had done his best he sat down again. This time with his legs well spread. He followed the progress of the rest of the drying mud with close attention.

It was in a fit state for brushing down to the last quarter square inch when he next consulted his watch. The time was seven fifty.

He completed his cleaning-up operation, which left his trousers looking crinkled and dirtyish but just presentable, and then went and put his head out of the door again. This time he caught a glimpse of a servant, not the smart bearer who had shown him in, but another man, lower in the scale though somewhere above the sweeper line. He was idling across the end of the corridor.

'Hoy,' Ghote called out.

The man stopped. Ghote beckoned. The man came forward, reluctantly but curiously.

'Do you know where your master is?' Ghote asked him.

The man, a skinny fellow of about sixty with an apologetic-looking grey moustache, half there and half shaved away, gave him a quick conspiratorial smile.

'He is waiting,' he said.

'Waiting? What for?'

'For the inspector from Bombay.'

'But I am the inspector from Bombay. Your master is waiting for me? Then take me to him.'

'Oh, no, sahib.'

'No? But why not?'

'He is not waiting to see you, sahib. I have heard him tell Moti, the head bearer, that you must be kept to wait a long time.'

He let the man, who seemed strongly nervous now though still friendly, go on his way and shutting the door behind him he settled down to wait. If the Chairman thought he was going to make him angry by humiliating him, then he was going to be proved wrong.

Half an hour passed.

Ghote was unable to remain sitting on the old sofa with the torn yellow covering. He began pacing about the room. He looked out of the door. Nothing. He looked out of the window. A striped cat, unusually fat and well-fed in appearance as if everything here was of a superior quality, was crouching under the branches of the margosa tree staring at a raggedy sparrow that had daringly alighted on the lawn not far away and was pecking at some of the little yellow flowers knocked down by the rain from the tree above.

The cat stared. The sparrow hopped. Ghote watched.

And then at last the sparrow, sensing perhaps that the cat was about to break the heavy calm of the dusk outside with a lion-like spring, suddenly flew off. The cat continued to crouch in the same tense position, but Ghote could see that the fire had gone out of her.

'Billi,' he called softly. 'Billi, billi.'

After a little the cat rose to its feet, turned and gave him a long look.

'Billi, billi, billi,' he called, thinking that a cat at least would while away the time.

The animal turned its head and stalked off, calm and disdainful, thick tail held perfectly upright. The last of the daylight vanished from the garden.

Ghote went over to the door of the room and switched on the light. The single naked bulb hanging, fly-blown, from the ceiling was of such low power that it gave only a pool of orangeish light right in the centre of the room.

For a quarter of an hour Ghote sat staring at it. Then he got up and opened the door again.

The servant who had let out the secret of why he had been kept waiting so long was standing outside.

'The master would not see you yet,' he said, and giggled.

Never mind, Ghote thought, at least the fellow will be company.

He beckoned him in and began to talk, asking the man such questions about himself and his affairs as came into his mind. The fellow replied happily enough, but evidently he possessed little capacity for initiating conversations of his own and each line of talk Ghote started soon petered into nothingness.

So it was not with the intention of furthering his case against Vinayak Savarkar that he asked the man whether he had been a servant here at the time the Chairman had married into the family. But the answer he got sent springing up in him a sharp flicker of hope.

'Oh yes, sahib, I was born in the servants' quarter of this house. When he came here with the other servants he had there was not much room for us.'

'Your master brought servants from his former home?' Ghote asked.

'Oh yes, sahib. Though they were not needed. Already Old Master had plenty.'

'But New Master brought more? How many?'

'Five, sahib. All very old.'

'Five.'

'They are dead now, sahib.'

'Dead?'

'One only is still living, the old woman who was nurse of the master's first wife.'

'And she is still living in this house?'

Ghote's excitement was rising.

'In the servants' quarters, sahib. She is blind and she does not leave there, but she is always wanting more than what is hers.'

'She is there now?' Ghote began. 'Tell me, can I come – '

He had been speaking, in his excitement, in quite a loud voice. And suddenly the door of the little room had been sharply opened.

It was the head bearer, Moti.

He said nothing. But the jerk of the head with which he sent his underling scurrying out spoke volumes. And, without a word to Ghote, the moment the man had left he turned and closed the door behind them both, firmly and decisively.

For a little while Ghote nurtured the thought of slipping out of the window, lurking among the branches of the margosa tree, finding out somehow where the servants' quarter was and then making a foray into it and getting hold of the old blind nurse. It was, after all, not impossible that she knew something about what had taken place in the Chairman's first home on that day fifteen years before when Mrs Sarojini Savarkar had suddenly died in pain. Perhaps she would not have anything amounting to proof of the Chairman's guilt. If she had, she would no longer be anywhere within reach at all, that was certain. But she might still know something that would give a pointer to something else. Probably it was for this very reason that she had been introduced into an already servant-crammed house and had been kept on there, blind and useless and complaining, all this time.

But the practical difficulties of getting to see her at this moment were really too great. Ghote got up and began walking up and down, through the patch of weak orangey light, into the darkness, turn, through the patch of light, into the other area of darkness, turn and back.

When at last he permitted himself one more look at his watch he realized that so much time had passed that there was a danger that in the middle of his interview with the Chairman, if he ever got it, Superintendent Chavan would come blundering in, intent on rescuing his made-off-with police colleague. He must telephone him at once.

And, he thought with a little puff of rosy pleasure, here was an excellent reason for leaving this terrible room.

He went over and opened the door briskly. He could see no one. Where would the telephone be? Would there be two or more in this big house?

He set off, jaunty as a schoolboy with an unexpected day's holiday, down the corridor in the direction of the entrance hall.

And, as he stepped clear of the end of the passageway, a voice spoke sharply, accusingly, at his elbow.

'Where are you going?'

A long pause and then 'Sahib, please.'

It was the head bearer.

Ghote reflected that he would not have got far if he had attempted to contact Sarojini Savarkar's old nurse.

'I am looking for a telephone,' he said. 'I did not expect to be here this long and I told my colleagues at the police-station that if I did not return they should come to find out where I was.'

No harm, he thought, in letting this fellow know he had taken his precautions, And, it seemed, this put a little respect into him too, because he answered in a plainly more subdued manner.

'There is only one telephone, sahib. It is in the hall. Be so good as to follow me.'

Ghote went with him to the black-and-white chequered hall, where Moti indicated the telephone standing on a small dark wood table inlaid with ivory. Ghote picked up the receiver. He noticed that Moti had made no attempt even to move a little out of hearing. He got hold of the police-station.

'Please inform Superintendent Chavan that my interview with Mr Savarkar has been delayed,' he said. 'Please tell that I do not know how late I shall be returning.'

He managed to inject a satisfactory degree of bitterness into these last words and laid the receiver down again feeling decidedly better.

Silently Moti led him back to the little waiting-room. And once again he sat for as long as he could endure on the yellow sofa. Then he paced, endlessly it seemed, in and out of the patch of orangey light once more. Finally in an excess of boredom he even explored the almirah with the sagging door.

It contained nothing but a Teddy-bear with a torn ear, doubtless left there by the unlikely offspring of the Chairman and his ugly wife.

It was more than an hour later that Moti appeared again.

'Mr Savakar will see you now, sahib,' he said.

9

The room in which Vinayak Savarkar received Inspector Ghote was on the first floor of the big house. It was evidently the office he used when he worked at home, a big heavily furnished room with a long balcony of intricately carved wood outside, visible to Ghote through the uncurtained windows against the dark backdrop of the night.

The Municipal Chairman himself sat, teeth clamped on a long thin cigar, at a large desk, on which there were a few papers, a large silver tray containing an array of sweetmeats, a silver cigar box and a big glass ashtray half full of squashed and mangled butts as well as an inlaid box containing all the equipment necessary for making luscious and expensive paans – though when he would find time to chew one of these what with his cigars and his sweetmeats Ghote could not imagine.

'Sit, sit, Inspector,' the Chairman said as Ghote was ushered in.

Ghote looked round about. In the immediate vicinity of the desk there was only one low cane-work stool. He glanced backwards to see if there was a chair he could boldly march over and collect. The only other seats in the room were great heavy leather armchairs, all far away.

'I prefer to stand,' he said.

'Sit, Inspector, sit when I say.'

Ghote decided that, rather than find himself in an argument over a triviality, he would sit. He lowered himself on to the drum-shaped stool. It was a long way down and his head when he was seated at last seemed to come only just to the top of the Chairman's desk so that he was forced almost to crick his neck even in order to be able to look the Chairman full in his birth-marked, teeth-flashing face.

'Mr Savarkar,' he said sharply, 'you know why I am here.'

'No,' the Chairman said, leaning back suddenly in the leather-padded chair of his desk. 'No, I do not know.'

Ghote fought back his anger.

'When I met you in your car two days ago,' he said, 'you knew well.'

The Chairman, his cigar back again between his teeth, said something in such a mumbled way that Ghote could not be sure what the words were.

'What was that, Mr Savarkar?' he asked tartly.

Now the cigar came out.

'I am saying you never met me in my car.'

'But I did. You know that is so.'

'It is not so.'

'But your driver, he was there. The tongawalla was there. They were witnesses to that discussion.'

'You may ask my driver, Inspector. You may ask the tonga-walla also. Ask all you want. They will tell that that talk never took place.'

Ghote realized he had to concede defeat.

'Very well,' he resumed, 'let me tell you that I am here to investigate the death of your late wife, Sarojini. And that I wish to question you with regard to the circumstances of that death.'

'But that is fifteen years ago. What should I remember?'

The cigar was removed again. The crocodile teeth flashed.

'Even after fifteen years have passed,' Ghote said, 'you must remember the way in which your wife died.'

'Yes, yes,' the Chairman said with sudden solemnity. 'That I remember. It was so sudden. She was in agony, poor woman. It was bad food she ate, you know.'

'The cause of her death was never properly established,' Ghote retorted. 'I have been examining the papers of the case.'

'And the papers are not saying it was bad food? Then they are making mistake.'

'No,' Ghote persisted. 'The question is considered to be open still because not enough evidence has been produced. And now I am seeking that missing evidence. And there are various matters I wish to draw to your attention.'

'Inspector, you are saying that it was by foul means my wife died?'

'I am saying there is every reason to suspect.'

'Then, Inspector, you must find the person who did this.

Justice must be done, Inspector. If my money can help you, it is there for you to ask for.'

'It is not your money I am wanting,' Ghote retorted, 'it is the truth from you.'

'The truth? If that helps to find this murderer you shall have the truth, Inspector.'

'Then,' said Ghote, pressing himself up an inch or two on his low stool and leaning forward, 'will you tell me for what purpose it was that you made air journey to Bombay and back on the day of your wife's death?'

This was his long shot. There had been only one chance reference in the reports to the Chairman's having returned from Bombay earlier on the day of the death, a mere phrase. But it had struck Ghote that if he was responsible for the death then it was very likely that he would have preferred to get hold of the poison in Bombay rather than locally.

It looked as if the shot might have gone home too. The Chairman slowly lowered his cigar and tumbled it still alight into the big ashtray.

'In Bombay?' he said, rather gropingly. 'But how do you know I was in Bombay on that day, Inspector?'

'It is in evidence,' Ghote said firmly.

'So you are certain?'

'I am certain.'

The Chairman leant back in his chair.

'Then let me tell you that I went to Bombay to buy a sari. To buy a sari for my much-loved wife, Inspector. Something very special, of nylon. You remember fifteen years ago, Inspector, a sari of imported nylon was something special. It was as a special present for my wife that I wanted that sari from Bombay.'

'Why did you want to give special present?' Ghote demanded still clutching hope.

'But, Inspector, because I greatly loved her.'

'Then what happened to that sari?'

'Inspector, when the woman I greatly loved died suddenly in horrible circumstances you expect me to remember what happened to a sari?'

'The woman you greatly loved,' Ghote retorted. 'But six months after her death you were married again already.'

'Yes, Inspector, it is so.'

'And you still say you greatly loved her?'

'But, Inspector, when one has known the joys of a good marriage, what would you expect one to do but to try to find again, and as soon as possible.'

The crocodile grin flashed down on Ghote on his low stool with brazen insolence.

Wearily he took up another thread.

'Mr Savarkar,' he said, 'if, as seems likely, your wife died by arsenical poisoning can you suggest when the said arsenic would have been administered?'

'By arsenical poisoning, Inspector? Is this so?'

'I believe it is.'

'You believe, only, Inspector. But you have proof also?'

'No,' Ghote admitted grimly. 'I have got no absolute proof. Yet.'

'But you will try to obtain, Inspector. Even though the body was unfortunately burned. For my sake you will try to obtain, yes?'

'I will try to obtain,' Ghote promised with ferocity.

'Good, good.'

The Chairman reached forward and began concocting himself a paan, carefully spreading out the betel leaf and taking from his paan-box a careful pinch of this and a judicious measure of that. He continued to do this while Ghote put his next questions.

'Mr Savarkar, let us assume that death did take place from arsenical poisoning. Your wife died at 2125 hours on the day in question. At about 1900 hours she had ingested according to the pathologist's report a large meal consisting of mutton, rice, curry, spices, and lime pickle. She ate this meal, according to witnesses from your household at that time, in the old-fashioned manner after her husband had finished eating himself.'

'That is so, that is so,' the Chairman agreed. 'My late wife was a lady of most old-fashioned principles.'

'And you yourself had finished all the lime pickle laid out at the beginning of the meal, and insisted that your wife fetched more before she ate?'

Ghote banged in the question sharply.

The Chairman paused to masticate smackingly his paan before answering.

'Such details I am not remembering, of course, Inspector,' he said. 'It is all long ago. But if you say, if you say. Certainly I am extremely fond of lime pickle.'

'I could ask your present wife if this is so, or your servants? I could ask this evening?' Ghote snapped, taking a small risk.

For a moment the Chairman did not answer. Then his teeth, now red-stained with betel juice, flashed again.

'Very fond of lime pickle I was formerly, Inspector,' he corrected himself. 'But no one makes like my late wife. You understand?'

'I understand,' Ghote replied.

He felt entitled to allow himself this small consolation of irony. He knew, however much longer he kept pressing the Chairman, that he had shot his bolt.

Standing outside the tall carved gates of the Chairman's house as the turbaned chaprassi scrapingly closed them, a new and very uncomfortable thought attached itself abruptly to the load of misery Ghote felt he already carried.

His attempt at approaching the house earlier in the evening in the full majesty of the town's most impressive taxi had left him without any means of transport back. He could, at the end of his interview, have asked the Chairman's permission to telephone for the taxi again. But that would have been a final drop of humiliation that he could not have brought himself to swallow. So now he was faced with a long walk through the darkness.

Not too much to complain about in that, though he was feeling tired enough. What had, however, really upset him was the thought that perhaps the long delay he had been subjected to before he had got to see the Chairman had not simply been designed to put him at a disadvantage. Perhaps it had been designed to make certain that it was as late and as dark as this before he left the house.

What had the Chairman's exact words been at that first encounter of theirs? 'Men who would not hesitate to set upon a perfectly innocent man in the street at night and beat the daylights out of him'? Something like that.

He looked up at the sky. There was not a star to be seen. The thick grey blanket of cloud must be hanging unbroken all over the town. And only behind it, to judge from the faint light that allowed him to make out looming objects here and there, was the moon shining brightly and serenely.

Resolutely he set out along the softly muddy road.

It was a rare experience for him nowadays to be out at night in a deserted area. Darkness itself he was well enough accustomed to. The law-breakers of Bombay carried out many of their activities after dusk and anyone wishing to catch them was used enough to being up all night. But in Bombay there were street lights, and even in those areas where the municipal blessings had been withheld there was always the occasional Petromax lamp as well as the glow the sky reflected from the pulsing neons and bright bulbs in the rest of the city.

Here there was nothing.

Only shapes emerging blackly from the almost as thick blackness all around them. And noises. Noises that it was not easy to account for.

That distant, but not very distant, howl. What was it? Ah, it was an owl. He remembered the sound they made quite clearly from his boyhood days.

It was not that he was afraid. Just uneasy.

Something plopped sharply and abruptly on to the muddy surface of the road just ahead, and involuntarily he came to a dead halt, his hands spread to either side of him ready to battle off he knew not what enemy.

And then he half-heard, half-saw the rapid movement of big wings and realized that it had only been a fruit bat, a flying fox, sweeping close overhead and letting fall some mangled fig or other fragment.

He walked forward more briskly.

After a little he found he was whistling a film song through his teeth. Well, did it matter? Surely a person was allowed to whistle?

Ahead in the darkness he thought he saw a tiny glimmer of light. It could be anything, he told himself.

It could be a lantern or an electric torch held behind a thick horny hand, another inner voice told him.

He found he was not walking anything like so fast, and that he had stopped whistling.

Then a sudden sweat of pure relief broke over him. Fireflies. There was a pulsating cluster of fireflies hovering over a roadside patch of what might be kika-thorn bushes. Had he forgotten what fireflies looked like? Was his boyhood all that long ago?

So why was he standing stock still?

He drew in a deep breath preparatory to setting out again. And at that moment, in the stillness, he heard them. And this time there could be no mistaking. On the road behind him a number of people, certainly two, perhaps four or even five, were advancing in his direction and taking great care not to make too much noise about it.

He found he was suddenly walking forward at a nice easy pace, looking from side to side as he went to see what advantages there might be for him in the lie of the land. He was still fairly far out of the town. Soon his heightened senses told him that a darker mass rising up to his right was the containing bund of the town water tank, which he had noticed on his way out when the taxi had broken down.

So he had a fair way to go before there were many houses about and the possibility of some help from the occasional street lamps which the town rose to. Should he try and run till he got to this comparative safety? Or should he chance breaking off somewhere?

Unfortunately he knew nothing of what lay in the darkness to either side, while the goondas following no doubt knew every inch of the country round about. But, on the other hand, if he kept to the road, they would know too just how long they could leave him before trying something.

The tank bund was a solid shape directly to his right now.

Quite suddenly he decided to take advantage of it. It provided a slight hill in an otherwise flat piece of countryside. By running quickly up the earthen slope of the bund to where, as he could now make out, a wire protective fence ran round the long and narrow shape of the tank he could get a good view of the men coming after him on the road below. To know just how many he had to deal with would be something.

No sooner said than done.

He took a few more paces along the road, carefully not altering his step. And then he swerved quickly to the right and ascended the steep slope of the bund at a crouching run.

At the top he flattened himself on the grassy earth close up against the wire mesh of the fence and looked downwards. He found he was able to make out at once the party that had been following him. There were four of them. Big men, as far as he could judge, and probably dressed only in shorts or loincloths. Two of them had white headcloths as well. The other two seemed to be bare-headed.

Four, he thought. Enough of them to spread well out if he made a break for it.

And now they seemed to have realized that their quarry had done something unexpected. They had stopped and were evidently having a muttered consultation.

Had he succeeded in evading them?

He looked down at the land to either side of the road. It was difficult to make out exactly how things lay, but it looked as though on the far side of the road there was a patch of scrubland. The blotchy shapes of low-growing bushes, probably more kika, seemed to be clear, intermixed with the faint gleam from a good many puddles. It was hardly the sort of territory through which someone who did not know their way could move without making a fair amount of noise.

So the goondas would work out that he had come up on to the bund.

He looked along the inside of the wire fence. Some twenty or twenty-five yards back down near the steps leading into the great still black pool of the water there was a small shelter, little more than a roof on four poles. And under that shelter, plain enough to see now in the intermittent flicker of sheet lightning that had broken out somewhere on the horizon, was the tank watchman fast asleep.

Ghote contemplated trying to wake him. But the noise he would have to make calling to him from this side of the fence would at once betray his location. And in any case the sort of fellow the town would employ to look after something as little necessary to guard as the tank would be an old man, past anything in the way of help.

He decided to let him lie. If he did wake him, it would only earn him a broken head.

He looked down at the goondas again. They were still conferring, but he could see that they were each in turn looking up at the slope of the bund now.

It would not be long.

He took a quick glance along the fence in the other direction. Perhaps if he were to run full out ...

His eye lit on a gap in the mesh, plain against the distant lightning.

He slowly raised himself to a crouching position and then made for the hole in the wire at a run, keeping as low as he could. He cursed the light khaki of his borrowed uniform.

And then he was through. On the far side of the fence the ground sloped slightly downwards till it came to the top steps of the tank, now, with all the rain, only a foot or two above the surface of the water. Ghote dropped down into the scanty cover the ground formed and waited, straining his ears and endeavouring not to breathe heavily, to see if he could hear what the goondas were doing now.

It was some little time, during which he thought he had once or twice caught the sound of low voices calling to each other, before he realized that there was a third person inside the boundaries of the tank.

There was the old sleeping watchman, and there was someone else.

Some fifty yards ahead of him, perhaps not as much, a slim white-clad figure stood on the topmost step of the tank, looking forwards and downwards at the black expanse of the water.

And no sooner had he taken in the presence of this person, than he realized what it was they were there for.

It was a not uncommon way of committing suicide, to take the plunge into the night waters of some half-deserted tank. If one was no swimmer – and here in the very centre of the Indian sub-continent by no means everyone would be able to swim – it was as good a way as any of ending a miserable life.

He watched the still, slim, shortish figure. And he wondered where his duty lay. In the ordinary way as a policeman he would have had no hesitation in approaching quietly such a figure as this and making sure that they did themselves no harm.

But at this moment? At this moment when there were four great muscled goondas waiting to attack him, and when to speak out loud would be inevitably to give away his presence? And there was not only his own safety to consider. He had been sent here to do a job, and if he were put into hospital for months, or left somewhere dead, that job would not get done.

Nor was it only a job.

Damn it, the Municipal Chairman had got away with one hell of a lot. He should not be allowed to get away with this.

In front of him down on the steps of the tank the slim white-clad figure suddenly stopped. When he straightened up Ghote was almost certain he could see a large white envelope that had been placed on the tank step. So it was definitely going to be suicide.

Ghote got to his feet in one quiet movement and walked quickly but very quietly over the soft ground of the bund top towards the still figure.

When he was within a couple of yards he saw to his surprise that it was a boy of only thirteen or fourteen that he was going to have to deal with. For a moment he paused, thinking hard.

Then he took a long pace forward, so that he could grab the boy's elbow if he had to. When he spoke it was very quietly as if he was coaxing a sacred animal into an enclosure.

'It is a dark night to be out,' he said.

The boy started so wildly that he almost lost hit footing.

'Who – Who – What – ' he babbled.

'I also am out in the dark,' Ghote said comfortably. 'It is a night for thinking.'

And for other activities, he added to himself. For an instant he contemplated trying to use this youngster as a shield to get himself to some place of safety. He seemed, from the good quality of his white bush-shirt and shorts, to come from some well-to-do family, probably with a house quite near. If he could lead the boy back there . . .

But even as the thought entered his mind he knew he would have to dismiss it. Goondas under the Chairman's orders would not be the sort to balk at the presence of a stripling like this, and the boy was likely to end up badly hurt as well.

'Yes,' the boy answered now, the first shock of his fright leaving him, 'yes, it is a time for thinking.'

There was a strong tinge of self-dramatizing youthful melancholy in the words. Ghote calculated that his task was already half done. But he ought, all the same, to see if he could find out exactly what the matter had been.

'You were thinking also?' he said to the boy, speaking in a slightly wondering, here-is-a-fellow-spirit tone and confident in the darkness that his uniform epaulettes would be invisible.

'I was thinking,' the boy said darkly.

'Of what were you thinking, I wonder. Of life . . . ? Of death . . . ?'

Ghote could have smiled, the boy reacted so exactly as planned. But more than half his thoughts were on a matter that did not bear smiling about.

'Yes,' the boy said, 'it was of death that I was thinking.'

Suddenly he stooped, snatched up the large envelope that he had placed on the granite tank step beside him and thrust it crumplingly into his trouser pocket. Ghote hastily pretended to be looking introspectively out across the dark water of the narrow tank. He wished he could have looked behind him at the skyline to see whether any dark figures were crossing it. But he did not want to draw the boy's attention to anything like that. If he was to get out of him what his particular trouble was, he would have to do so in what seemed the complete secrecy of the night.

Now it was his own turn to drop a slow remark into the meditative atmosphere.

'Often,' he said, 'I have longed for death.'

He had been going to add ' . . . like a lover longing for his mistress.' But the youngster seemed a bit young for such a comparison.

'You also?' the boy said now, turning quickly to Ghote.

'Yes,' Ghote replied, still the mysterious philosopher. 'There are times in every man's life when Death seems the solution to so many troubles.'

'True, true,' commented his fellow-thinker.

'But then,' Ghote went on, after a proper pause, 'sometimes there is another answer.'

'Another answer?'

'Sometimes there comes into a man's life, mysteriously, he knows not from where, a kindred spirit. And there lies the other way.'

The boy had turned fully to face him now. His mouth was hanging a little open. The words were ready to drop out of it as a plum at its moment of ripeness falls from the tree. It was almost comic. Except that when the words had fallen there would be another, and not so easily solved, problem to be dealt with.

And except that for the boy this too had been a matter of life and death.

'May I speak to you?' the boy said now.

'Speak.'

'I am going to be married.'

This was not quite what Ghote had been expecting. An examination failure had been more the line his thoughts had travelled on.

'Married?' he said. 'But you cannot yet be fifteen.'

'I am fourteen just. But, you know, the law can be got round if the father is determined.'

Ghote did know.

'And you do not wish to marry?' he asked. 'You have seen the girl? She is not pretty?'

'She is very pretty.'

Again Ghote felt he had anticipated too much.

'But . . . ?' he asked tactfully.

Suddenly the boy jerked away from him.

'Oh, you would not understand,' he burst out.

Damn, Ghote thought, I have let him go.

He was half tempted to let him go in earnest. He knew that it needed only the slightest wrong answer on his part to have the lad storm off into the darkness now. And if he did that it would give the goondas, who almost certainly had by now heard their voices and were waiting for developments, a few minutes less in which to take up their positions, a few minutes which might make a lot of difference.

But in front of him was a tormented young man, and it was more than probable that his torment was one of the self-inflicted ones of youth.

Ghote addressed himself to the immediate task again. He recalled his own adolescence. And almost as if his mind had been lit up by the distant flash of lightning that at that moment broke in the distance – showing him up more clearly to the waiting goondas? – he found he knew what the answer was.

He spoke softly to the boy.

'Have you ever seen a baby being born?' he asked.

The boy's gasp came clear on the thick night air.

'How did you know it was that?' he said.

'You saw it. Perhaps you peeped through the walls of a hut when some woman in the servants' quarter of your house was giving birth. You thought even it was something dirty. And you found it was cries and pain?'

'Yes,' the boy whispered. 'And I am not going to make that happen to any woman. Ever.'

Ghote almost smiled in the darkness, only he was afraid the boy might catch a glimpse of his face and feel hurt. The very same experience had happened to him at much this age. And how long had the same implacable resolution he had made lasted? Perhaps a year. Just long enough for the process of growing-up to readjust him.

Yet he had not contemplated suicide. He must say something to this boy to help him break up the hollow burden he had placed upon himself. But what?

That after the pain of the birth the mother was always so

content that she had brought a child into the world that all the agony was forgotten? No. More than likely the boy had heard that one, and had rejected it.

'Listen,' he said, feeling his way a little. 'Listen, it is true that the pains of birth are often so hard that they make a woman cry out. But that – do you know the saying there is about this? Old sayings are good things. They are what people have thought concerning the problems that have come to them, just the same, for thousands and thousands of years. Do you know the saying we have about a birth?'

'No,' said the boy cautiously.

'A child is not born without blood,' Ghote said. 'And children must be born, you know. That cannot stop. And it cannot be done without blood. Without blood, remember that.'

He waited to see whether he would need to say any more.

There was a long silence while the boy thought at the problem. Then he spoke again.

'Thank you,' he said feelingly. 'And, good night.'

'Good night,' Ghote said.

He watched the white-clad boy walk away through the darkness along towards the gap in the wire fence through which he himself had come. He calculated that the goondas, seeing him going, would do nothing until he was out of hearing.

10

They came just exactly as Ghote had expected. He could almost have said 'One, two, three, go' before they started to move when the last sounds of the boy's footsteps had died away down on the road below.

Ghote saw the four of them quite easily. They were making no attempt at concealment now. They had no need to. He was standing right down by the edge of the black strip of water, and while he had been in conversation with the boy the four of them had come through the gap in the wire only fifteen yards away and had spread out in a line. They must have lain down in their prefixed positions and then when the boy was safely out of the way they had all stood up at the same time, like so many figures in a fairground booth.

Only Ghote was not going to shy anything at them. They were going to deal with him.

They advanced together, keeping in line. One of them was chuckling to himself, throatily.

Ghote waited. He could not see anything that he could do. The water of the tank lay only a foot or two behind him, stretching away to either side for perhaps a hundred yards in each direction. If he started to run along its edge one way or the other, the oncoming goondas would have to increase their pace only a little to trap him well before he got beyond the end of their line.

He licked his lips.

Now the two end men of the line were closing in more quickly. The two in the middle were only six or seven yards away from him but they had come to a halt and were standing there grinning. He could see white teeth clearly in the darkness.

The two at the far ends of the line had now reached the water's edge and were coming towards him that way. There was an abrupt sound from one of them and an outbreak of cursing. Evidently, in keeping his eyes intently on his target, he had put a foot wrong, slipped on the damp stone of one of the tank steps and had nearly gone in.

But even this mishap proved to be a measure of their confidence. The man plainly felt himself at leisure to have a thorough curse and swear about how nearly he had gone into the detested water before he got down to business.

How nearly he had gone into the detested water. Suddenly Ghote swung right round and without an instant of hesitation dived into the still and black tank.

He felt the cold rain-freshened water close about his body. Then his outstretched hands touched lightly against the slimed-over lower steps.

One peril safely behind. The steps had descended as steeply as the boy's suicide scheme had hinted that they might, and the escape plan had not come to an abrupt end with himself lying stunned in a foot of water.

Would his other assumption pay off as well? He struck out strongly, waiting to surface only till he was out of easy stone-throw range. And then he swam just as hard as he could, and he listened.

The goondas on the bank were shouting to each other, loud and angry Marathi voices.

And, yes, they were shouting what he had dared to hope they would. They were shouting to each other to run round the long and narrow tank. Not one of them could swim. The man who had slipped on the edge and had been so put out by what had nearly happened to him had spoken for them all. Here, almost in the centre of India, by no means everyone was a swimmer.

The far side of the narrow tank loomed up out of the darkness. The goondas' shouts sounded far off.

But he would hurry all the same until he had got right to the safety of the police-station. There was going to be much to do next day and he was not going to take the least risk of not being there to do it.

In spite of having returned with borrowed uniform clinging soddenly after its immersion in the tank and in spite of the discomforts of a night on an improvised bed in Inspector Popatkar's office, next morning Ghote felt wonderfully invigorated. The Municipal Chairman had failed once: he was not then invariably successful in his undertakings as everybody liked to make out.

Now it remained to take advantage of this failure.

It was as likely as not, Ghote calculated, that the goondas were being careful to go to ground after letting him escape. No one would like telling the Municipal Chairman that they had not succeeded in carrying out orders he had given them. So, as far as the Chairman was concerned, the intrusive inspector from Bombay was out of the way. Now was the time to strike then. And the place to strike was obvious too. At the Chairman's very house. There was the old nurse from his first wife's home there somewhere in the servants' quarter and, from the way she had been hidden, it was certainly possible that she had something to tell.

Ghote waited until the Chairman was bound to have come into his office in the centre of the town, and then he went and had a quick precautionary word with Superintendent Chavan before setting out.

'I shall go there dressed once more as a chicken-feed sales representative,' he said to him. 'Thank goodness, no one in the town seems to have linked that man with the police inspector from Bombay yet.'

Superintendent Chavan glanced down at the considerable expanse of his beautifully ironed uniform.

'Yes, yes,' he said. 'In certain branches of our work disguise is undoubtedly necessary.'

'Quite so, sir, quite so,' Ghote agreed. 'And that is why I would be obliged if you would issue an order to your men in the station here to take particular pains not to mention what my present appearance is. And also I am telling only you each day where I shall be going.'

'First-class idea,' said the superintendent.

And, those ringingly confident tones still in his ears, Ghote set out with his brightly labelled egg-box on the rear carrier of his battleship bicycle for the Chairman's house once more.

His journey seemed to be going to take place under good auspices too. As he pushed his way past the Post Office, he saw that the banner with the words GHOTE GO on it had been allowed to fall sideways and had not been picked up. Its brightly white material was bedraggled and mud-stamped.

Had any emissary from the Chairman yet told the Swami as he embarked on the sixty-third day of his fast that Inspector Ghote was no longer causing trouble in the town, he wondered. Probably not. The Chairman would want a circumstantial account of what had happened to him before allowing this news to go running through its swift channels out to the ruined temple and those ashen hair-hidden ears. And no doubt too *Time* magazine would still be ignorant that it's 'Saint-v-CID' story was supposed to have come to an abrupt end.

Swinging round a particularly deep and large puddle in the roadway, Ghote smiled to himself.

He was still smiling a little when he arrived outside the heavy carved wooden gates of the compound of the Chairman's house, after a short halt not far away to conceal his egg-box just inside the big patch of fan-leaved kika thorns where the fireflies had hovered the night before. He called out loudly to the turbaned chaprassi to open up as he had done on his visit in state the evening before.

But now he got a very different reception.

The tall burly figure surveyed him disdainfully through the thick carving of the gates.

'What is it you are wanting?' he demanded.

'I have come to carry out certain interviews in the house,' Ghote replied briskly.

'And you are permitted to come interviewing here?' answered the chaprassi with a coarse scorn which Ghote decided he could not possibly ignore.

He drew himself up to his full height, impeded only a little by the necessity of holding his bicycle.

'I am Inspector Ghote of the Bombay CID,' he said. 'You will open these gates immediately.'

But the chaprassi made no move. Instead he leant back a little and carried out a leisurely survey both of Ghote and his means of transport.

'You are police inspector?' he said at length. 'Then I am brothel girl.'

The expression he had hit on evidently pleased him. He relaxed his lofty stance to smile broadly at the gardeners and other servants whom Ghote could see beyond the thick gates creeping one by one nearer to enjoy the spectacle of a suppliant being sent away at the gates.

Ghote saw that the whole dignity of the police was at stake. He did not hesitate.

'Get those gates open, man,' he shouted in a sudden violent blast of sound. 'Get them open pretty damn quick, or you will find yourself in gaol.'

It was as if he had fired a gun through the solid wood carvings in front of him. The tall chaprassi positively cowered. Then he swung round to the small crowd of servants.

'Get away back to your work,' he yelled at them. 'Get away this instant. Inspector Ghote is coming.'

And with a salaam of the utmost courtliness he applied himself to the business of dragging back both halves of the heavy gates for Ghote's entrance, while inside the compound a scurry of terrified servants – there was even, Ghote saw, a footless cripple wildly swinging a pair of crutches – shot away in all directions as if a tiger had been dropped down among a flock of goats.

'Take my bicycle,' Ghote said to the chaprassi. 'And see that it is well looked after.'

'Yes, sahib. Of course, sahib,' the man said, reverently wheeling the machine away.

Ghote walked solemnly and alone up the immaculately swept drive to the door of the house.

And it seemed that the fracas at the gate had alerted the whole house to his arrival. When he was within five yards of the wide door it swung respectfully back and Moti, the head bearer, appeared.

'Good morning, Inspector sahib,' he said. 'Madam is here to see you.'

Ghote, inwardly a little disappointed to find that his tentative plans for getting into the servants' quarter in one taking-all-before-him rush had come unstuck, inclined his head gravely and entered the spacious marble-chequered entrance hall.

Very well, he reflected, I shall just have to go about the business in another way.

He felt, comfortingly, the fresh impulse that his outwitting of the goondas had given him still filling his sails, freshened if anything by his brush with the chaprassi at the gates.

The second Mrs Savarkar, who was waiting for him at the far end of the hall, was certainly every bit as ugly as Superintendent Chavan had said. Despite her sari of bright green silk, her large gold earrings and the numerous gold and silver bangles she wore on both arms, she looked like a man. She had close-set eyes, one of which seemed to be subject to squint, a large aggressively beaky nose, a little downward-turning mouth, and putting all the rest into comparative insignificance, a real boxer's jaw.

'Well, well, Inspector,' she said sharply, 'what is it that you are doing here? My husband is at office. You ought to be knowing that.'

'It was not your husband I came to see, Mrs Savarkar,' Ghote replied soothingly.

'Not my husband? Then who is it you have come for? We cannot be having police here at whatever time they choose.'

'I quite understand, madam,' Ghote replied. 'But my inquiries will not take long, and they are chiefly concerned with someone who, I understand, no longer has any duties in the household.'

'What is this? What is this? Who no longer has duties in this household?'

Mrs Savarkar's formidable jaw bit at her questions savagely.

'It is the former nurse of Mr Savarkar's first wife I am wishing to see,' Ghote admitted with some reluctance.

'What person is this? Former wife? Former wife? It is fifteen years now since I am married to Mr Savarkar. What is this former wife?'

'Yes, I quite understand that you have been married for a long time,' Ghote said placatingly, since it was very plain that Mrs Savarkar took great pride in her marital status, and no wonder.

He coughed apologetically.

'But Mr Savarkar was married before he became your husband,' he added. 'And I understand that the nurse of his first wife came with him to this house. It is her I wish to speak with.'

'There is no such person,' Mrs Savarkar stated abruptly.

Ghote drew in a breath.

'I regret,' he said, 'but it is my distinct information that such a person exists, and I require to see her in connection with inquiries.'

Mrs Savarkar shrugged her bony-ridged shoulders, displacing a little the vivid sari. Hastily she drew it back into position, as if it would be grossly unfair to any man to expose him to the least bit more of her charms than convention dictated.

'But she will tell you nothing,' she said.

'Nevertheless,' Ghote replied, 'it is my duty to see.'

'She is blind only. What can she tell you?'

'But she was not blind fifteen years ago. And it is the events of that time I am investigating.'

'She knows nothing of that.'

'Nevertheless she was a member of the household in which a certain tragic event occurred. She was an intimate member even. I would like to see her at once.'

Mrs Savarkar hitched at her sari impatiently.

'Oh see, see,' she said. 'She can tell you nothing.'

She darted Ghote a glance of confident triumph.

Ghote, secretly agreeing that since the old woman had not been sent away to the remotest corner of India it was pretty likely that she would not in fact have anything really helpful to say, felt obliged nevertheless to stand his ground.

'Kindly have the goodness,' he said stiffly, 'to have me taken to see her.'

And it looked as if he had won his probably empty victory too, because Mrs Savarkar turned towards the silent Moti, who had placed himself beside the telephone on its ivory-inlaid table, and began telling him to escort Ghote to the servants' quarter.

But before she had finished a door into the hall opened abruptly, and Mrs Savarkar, when she saw who was there, swung round again to Ghote, not without showing some relief.

'Aha,' she said, 'it is my little son, my Vasant. First you must talk with him.'

Ghote, beginning to worry once more that the old nurse with whom his interview was once more being delayed might after all have something to tell him, turned ungraciously to appraise the fruit of the Savarkar union now coming, a little reluctantly, into the hall.

He found he was confronting the boy he had met at the tank.

11

Ghote stood stock still looking at the boy, so surprised that he could not think what to do or say.

He had somehow imagined that the offspring of the Savarkar union was still very young, and to find that he was this adolescent, and one with whom he had had such an intimate conversation, was altogether disrupting.

And what thoughts must be tumbling through young Vasant's head? Here was the mysterious, anonymous stranger in whom he had confided his innermost secrets revealed not merely as a real person actually present in his own home, but as the very inspector of police sent to harass his own father, a sworn enemy.

In his own young days, he knew, he would have wanted the ground to open and swallow him up. And, in default of this ideal solution, he would have at least turned and fled and have hidden away for as long as he possibly could.

He must say something. It was up to him to make the situation tolerable.

'Good morning,' he grated out, his voice sounding to his ears impossibly strained. 'I am most pleased to make your acquaintance.'

That should do it, he thought. At least it makes it clear that the incident of the night before is blotted out.

Vasant, staring at him as if he had lost the power of movement, made no reply. And he was struggling to concoct another remark of his own when he was saved from further effort by a sudden sharp shout somewhere outside.

'Where is he? Where is that man?'

He recognized the voice at once. It was the Municipal Chairman. He knew too without having to be told who 'that man' was. It was himself.

'Inspector Ghote,' he shouted. 'They are telling me you are here. And straightaway I am coming.'

Ghote felt trapped. He had no strict right to be here at all.

All he could find to say were the same words with which he had greeted the Chairman's son.

'Good morning.'

'For you,' the Chairman replied, with a crocodile flash of his white teeth above the boat-shaped birth mark, 'it is not a good morning. You have come to my house without authority. You are trying to question my servants when you have no right. You are in trouble, Inspector.'

'If necessary I will obtain search warrant,' Ghote replied, all the more hotly for knowing how weak his case was.

'Apply, Inspector, apply,' the Chairman answered. 'But in this town you will not find it so easy to get. And now, since you have not warrant, you will leave.'

And all Ghote could do, knowing he had been utterly defeated, was to go. He went down the steps outside the front door of the big house and along the beautifully-kept driveway. He took his bicycle from the chaprassi, who was contriving to hold it upright while touching it with only one finger. Then he wheeled the desperately heavy machine out of the tall carved gates of the compound, all the while conscious of the eyes of the Chairman, his wife, his son and his servants upon him.

Trudgingly he pushed the machine along the whole length of the high mud-wall surrounding the Chairman's establishment and on until he reached the patch of kika thorn where he had hidden his egg-box. And there he stood while the heat from the glaring grey sky twanged down at him and savoured his setback to its last bitter drop.

The Chairman had won again. How quickly the situation had changed. First thing this morning he had felt himself in a totally superior situation: he had been supposed dead or at least beaten senseless and he was priding himself on having grabbed all the advantages that that situation had given him. And now . . . Now the Chairman had won again. He had defied the expected course of events and had come tearing out back to his house to dismiss like a beggar a man who was making a nuisance of himself.

Ghote stood under the grey glare of the sky and let the misery seep through and through him.

So it must have been quite a long time before the persistent voice registered with him.

'Inspector. Inspector. Inspector, please.'

But at last the hissed sound penetrated. He looked round a little wildly, jerking sharply back to the present.

There seemed to be nothing, no one.

His already sweating back broke out in a fresh upswelling. What was happening to him?

And then he saw what it was. At the far side of the scrubby patch of kika-thorn, there was someone crouching, a figure wearing white. He took a step nearer to see if he could discover whom it was.

'Inspector, come round this side. We can talk with no one to see.'

Ghote hesitated for a moment. Was this a trap? Had the Chairman already set a new lot of goondas on to him?

And then he realized quite suddenly whom the mysterious whisperer was. It was young Vasant.

Quickly he scrambled down from the road, through a narrow path in the thorns and round to where the boy crouched.

'You were calling?' he said.

'Yes, Inspector, there is something important I must tell.'

Ghote forced himself to take an interest. Bowed down he might be with the heavy weight of his repeated failure to best the Chairman, but, after all, no doubt to the boy his own worries seemed as weighty. So he would have to listen with attention to a plea not to tell anybody of what had happened at the tank the night before, and solemnly accede to a request that never need have been made.

'Well, what is it you want?' he said gravely.

'Inspector, it is the Swami.'

'The Swami?'

For a moment Ghote scarcely knew what Vasant was talking about so unexpected was this reply. Then, when he realized whom the boy was speaking of, all his former bitterness came rushing back to him. What was this child doing poking his nose into a man's business? The Swami represented the Chairman's most successful attempt to prevent any investigation of the case. Why was this boy thrusting him down his throat now?

'What is it? What is it you have to tell?' he said testily.

The boy, crouching in the shadow of the thorn patch, took a long deep breath.

'Inspector,' he said, 'do you know who the Swami is?'

'Who he is?' Ghote said impatiently. 'He is a holy man. He came to the town some years ago. The people listen to him. He is telling them that I must go.'

'But do you know who he is, Inspector?'

Ghote realized that he did not in fact know the holy man's name. He doubted very much if more than a handful of people in the whole town did, if that. It was enough that he was a holy man.

'No,' he said. 'No, I do not know his name. What importance is that?'

The boy looked up at him, his eyes wide with the overriding importance of what he had to say. And what would it be? Nothing.

'Inspector, his name is Gandharva, the same name as my grandfather. Inspector, he is my grandfather's brother.'

Ghote stood leaning over young Vasant rapidly working out the consequences of what the boy had told him.

So the Swami was a relative by marriage of the Municipal Chairman. He was, if what the boy had said was true, the brother of the former Chairman, the man who had lacked a son to pass on his power and wealth to and had caused Vinayak Savarkar to murder his wife in order that he could marry the ugly daughter who was his sole offspring. And if this was so, then what a hold it was for him to have over the Swami. It would be necessary only to tell him that this relationship was known to have him call off his long campaign at once.

He straightened up and brushed a hand across his sweat-globuled face.

'It is not generally known, this relationship?' he asked the boy.

'No, no. My father always wanted it kept most secret. The Swami would always tell him he was a wicked man. And he

99

knew that if people heard he was disobeying his own wife's uncle they would think he was very wicked.'

'And so how did it happen that the Swami protected your father?' Ghote asked.

'My father went to him.'

'Went to him? He went to beg the Swami's help?'

This was getting better and better.

'Yes,' the boy said, 'when my father got to know that the people in Bombay were determined to have him thrown out of office and the way they were planning to do it he went to the Swami for help. He knew that if it was the Swami who was objecting to the investigation then he himself could not be accused of obstructing. He is a very clever man, you know.'

'I know,' Ghote said. 'But, tell me, why did the Swami agree to do it? You said he did not approve of your father.'

'It is true. That is why my father had to go to him himself, in secret. And even then he had to beg and beg. But the Swami is a relative after all.'

'Yes,' Ghote said.

And he saw the force of the boy's statement. There was an obligation to help one's family in this world. Look at the Eminent Figure in Bombay insisting that he himself went round this distant town with that brightly coloured egg-box. That was helping your family. And the Swami's action was no more. It was understandable. But it would be easy enough to stop now.

Suddenly Ghote came back to the boy sitting at his feet.

'But you,' he said. 'Will your father realize you have told me this? They must know you went out at the house. There is only the one gate to go through, isn't there?'

The boy looked at his sandal-shod feet.

'Yes,' he said, 'there is one gate only, and they will know. But I do not care.'

'But if your father hears, he will make trouble for you. He is not a man to cross.'

The boy looked up at him now.

'Already he has made much trouble,' he said. 'Though I do not so much mind doing what he says I must now. I have been thinking about what you said last night.'

'Well,' Ghote replied, 'you have helped me a great deal at a bad time for me. Thank you.'

The boy looked up at him in silence.

He decided that it was time to go. The information he had learnt was boiling up inside him waiting to be used.

He retrieved the bright orange egg-box, dodged his way out of the kika-thorn patch and strapped it on to his bicycle. Then, pressing his feet on the thick pedals for all he was worth, he started off for the river road. He was going to have a very different sort of interview this time with the irascible holy man.

He drove the ironclad machine along the road, careless of whether he was sending up great shoots of water from the puddles or not. And as he rode he rearranged in his mind all the events of his stay in the town in the light of his new knowledge.

He was definitely on top once again. The Chairman might have managed to overcome the disadvantage of his goondas' failure, he might have managed to get out to his house so quickly that he had stopped any line of investig –

Abruptly Ghote's thoughts came to a full stop. His feet ceased to turn the bicycle pedals. How had the Chairman got out there so quickly? There had not been time for anyone to have gone to give him a warning, since even the fastest cyclist would not have succeeded in getting all the way into the town centre in between his own arrival and that of the Chairman barely ten minutes later. And no warning could have been given by telephone either. As it happened Moti had told him on his previous visit that there was only one instrument in the house, and he himself had been within sight of it the whole time of his visit. So how . . . ?

And he knew the answer almost before he had formulated the question.

He had told one person and one person only where he was going. He had even stressed the importance of not spreading the information. So that one person must have got straight on to the Chairman to warn him that the Bombay inspector was going out to his house on a promising line of investigation. No doubt this person would have asked the Chairman to be discreet about how he dealt with matters, but the Chairman, scorning anything cautious, had simply jumped into his big car and had driven out to the house as fast as he could.

And that person was, of course, Superintendent Chavan.

The bicycle had meanwhile drifted almost to a halt on the muddy surface of the road. Ghote swung it round by main force and set out again as fast as he could go, in the direction of the police-station.

But he was not to get there without trouble. As he entered the broad main street he saw that a crowd was gathered in front of the station itself. And from the shouts that arose occassionally it was only too plain that it was an angry crowd.

Cautiously Ghote brought his lumbering bicycle to a halt and advanced on foot, wheeling it beside him. Before he had gone many yards he saw that between the smartly whitewashed exterior of the police-station and the crowd a line of half a dozen police constables was drawn up. Each was armed with a long bamboo lathi and was waving it threateningly.

Ghote squished through the slush of the street till he had got even nearer. Then he was able to confirm something he had seen at a distance, and had not at all liked. The expressions on the faces of the constables were all similar: they looked like men who were decidedly scared.

At any moment, Ghote realized, the crowd was likely to launch itself forward. Men as experienced in local trouble-making as the constables would know from the signs that this was no holiday bust-up. These particular trouble-makers meant business.

And it did not need the sudden hoisting of the mud-spattered banner on its two long poles to tell him what the anger, rising up from the crowd like steam from a boiling pot, was directed against. As clearly as the smeared letters on the banner, it spelt 'Ghote Go'.

The Chairman was certainly a fast worker.

No sooner had he himself left the compound of the man's house than he must have been on the telephone sending some trusted hireling from his office out into the streets to stir up trouble.

For a little Ghote was tempted to get on his bicycle and quietly pedal off, round the edge of the town, back on to the river road and out to the ruined temple and the Swami. But he realized that nothing he could do immediately would cause the trouble to calm down. The Chairman had had it stirred up: it would be with them all the rest of the day.

In the meantime would it still be possible to get into the police-station by the back way?

He remounted and set off cautiously down a narrow lane between the Krishna Bhavan Restaurant and the Co-operative Bank. The sound of the crowd's rising and falling shouts of protest fading as he penetrated farther along the lane with its squawking scrawny chickens (how much they would benefit from Grofat chicken-feed) and its scratching mangy dogs. Soon he found himself in the ordure-smelling area at the back of the police-station compound where there was still no sign of an angry crowd.

He dismounted thankfully from his weighty steed and rattled at the narrow rusty gate.

A constable came across the compound at a run, waving a lathi and all set to repel boarders. But as soon as he recognized Ghote he produced the long key to the gate and let him in, preceding him afterwards to Superintendent Chavan's office with all the pride of a drum major.

As they went, the excitements of avoiding the angry crowd, whose shouts could hardly be heard here at the back of the police-station building, swirled away out of Ghote's mind and left in their place only the residue of his discovery about the superintendent.

A prickle of anger went through him.

How completely he had been cheated. All the plans he had so eagerly discussed with this colleague of colleagues. All the help he had so gratefully accepted as from one policeman to another. All the trust he had put in the man's so evident pride in his uniform and his calling. And the whole time his own every move, his every thought no doubt, had been relayed as quickly as possible to the grinning figure of the Municipal Chairman.

And how diabolically he had been encouraged to go here and there about the town when it had been well known in advance that his errands were bound to be fruitless. Look at the way he had been allowed to learn that pensioned Ram Dhulup was a creature of the Chairman's. Of course he could be told that: Ram Dhulup had already been spirited away.

And no wonder that on that very first day of inquiries a man had been walking in the direction of Bhatu the basket-maker's hut with a copy of the newspaper containing a story about the Swami. No doubt that paper had been shown to each one of the members of the Coroner's Committee to remind them where their interests lay. There had certainly been a copy on chubby little Mr Pendharkar's desk.

He should have worked out from that that there had been a spy signalling his every move.

To the bewildered surprise of the police constable he pushed swiftly past him and burst into the superintendent's office unannounced.

The superintendent was standing by the window smoking a cigarette and looking out on to the compound, smoothing down the front of his already smooth uniform in his reflection in the window glass.

'Superintendent Chavan,' Ghote said in loud accusing tones, 'you have been telling my every plan to the Chairman.'

Superintendent Chavan looked just for a moment as if he had been struck in the face. But very quickly any such violent reaction was stifled. He turned back to the window again, leaning forward and peering as if in the poor reflection of the glass he was not able to see as much detail on his uniform as he would have liked.

Ghote drew himself up.

'It is of no use to deny,' he said. 'I told you and you only that I was going to the Chairman's house this morning, and hardly had I arrived than he was there saying he knew I had come.'

He glared so hard, and left such a pause in the air that the superintendent had no option but to turn round.

'My dear chap,' he said, brushing the air away in front of

him as if it was somehow distorting a plain situation, 'my dear chap, there must be some error.'

'Can you suggest how error occurred?' Ghote demanded. 'I most emphatically requested you to keep the information to yourself. Did you spread it round the station?'

'My dear fellow, of course not. Confidential information is confidential information.'

The superintendent looked shocked. The basis of his official life had been attacked.

'Very good,' Ghote said. 'Then if the information was not spread round the station, how does it happen that it came to the ears of the Chairman within minutes of my departure?'

'I can offer no suggestion,' said the superintendent.

He went and sat at his desk in a deflated way.

'Well, I can offer suggestion,' Ghote said brutally. 'The only possible explanation is that you have been in the Chairman's pay all along.'

'It is not a question of pay,' the superintendent said.

'Very well, I withdraw that. It is not a question of pay. But it is a question of friendship. You have put your friendship with a man of so much influence in the town before your duty as a police officer.'

'No, no, it is not so.'

The superintendent's denial was pathetic rather than vigorous. His hand went out to the braided cap resting in its usual position on the right hand side of the desk by the big brass ashtray.

'But you cannot deny facts,' Ghote banged out. 'I told you where I was going in confidence, and in no time at all the Chairman is there denouncing.'

He went and stood in front of the desk. Glaring down, demanding an answer.

'It is possible, I suppose,' the superintendent said glumly.

'Possible,' Ghote stormed. 'Nothing else is possible. I have been betrayed by the colleague I counted on.'

The superintendent positively clutched at his cap.

'Not betrayed,' he said.

'What other word is there?' Ghote shouted. 'What possible explanation can you offer?'

The superintendent looked up out of the corner of his heavy face.

'There is one possibility,' he suggested.

'What possibility is that?'

The superintendent got to his feet. He straightened his large, rather pudgy shoulders.

'Inspector,' he said. 'The Chairman was never guilty of the murder of his wife.'

12

Ghote felt as if his whole frame of reference was being held high, about to be smashed to pieces.

Could this be so? What had Superintendent Chavan got hold of?

'But the missing organs from the body?' he stammered. 'Why if he is not guilty were these concealed?'

The superintendent drew in a deep breath.

'Who is to say that it was poor Savarkar who was responsible for their disappearance?' he said. 'It may have been some error only.'

Ghote had to agree that it was not strictly proven that it had been the Chairman who had made away with the organs. He searched round in his mind for more conclusive proof.

'But his visit to Bombay as soon as he had heard the old Chairman say he wished he could have been his son-in-law?' he questioned. 'It seems to me this was most likely for the purposes of obtaining arsenic from some dispensary somewhere in the suburbs, some rundown place he must have known about. There are quite a few of those, I assure you, and I am seeing that investigations are made.'

But the superintendent nodded his head in bland negative.

'Again, what could be more of a supposition that that this Bombay visit was for such purposes?' he asked.

But Ghote was by no means done yet.

'Very well,' he replied, 'if the missing organs are the result of a mistake, and if that visit to Bombay was even as he said to purchase a sari as a gift, why all the same did he see that the pathologist who carried out post-mortem – what is his name, Adhikari – why did he see Adhikari was sent away to Nagaland? Because he knew that he might speak.'

He challenged the superintendent with it.

The superintendent spread his hands in a broad explanatory gesture.

'Of course he must take every precaution to see that if possible nothing was ever made public about the death being from poison,' he replied. 'If it was known that it was so, who else but he as her husband would be accused? Even if he was found Not Guilty at a trial, all would say it was he who had killed her.'

Ghote considered it. It was an answer. He had to admit.

'And it was for that reason all the agitation against me has been going on?' he felt obliged to ask.

'No doubt, no doubt,' the superintendent conceded.

'And for the same reason the Chairman hid away Ram Dhulup, the person on the Coroner's Committee who was representing his interests?'

'I am not in his confidence,' Superintendent Chavan replied magnanimously.

'But why then did you tell him where I was this morning?' Ghote burst out, a spark of indignation flying up from the ashes of his despair.

The superintendent leaned forward across his wide desk.

'Inspector,' he said. 'Understand my position. When you leave the town, he will still be here.'

'But no,' Ghote began to protest.

And then the thought struck at him that in all probability that would be the position. The Chairman would leave the town only if he was arraigned on a murder charge, and successfully. Nothing less would shift him. And how likely was it that he could be outmanoeuvred? Every time it had looked as if he was being so he had proved to possess a longer arm by far than a mere visiting inspector of police. So who was the more likely to be beaten in the end?

'Yet if he is murderer all the same,' he advanced, 'it is your duty to assist in bringing him to trial.'

Superintendent Chavan sat bolt upright and squared his puffy shoulders.

'Inspector,' he said, outrage billowing out from him in clouds. 'Inspector, do you think if I truly suspected that he had done this crime I would not in every way assist? No Inspector, it has all along been clear to me that Mr Savarkar is a much wronged man. Can you blame me for not wishing to incur his displeasure?'

'But,' said Ghote, 'if he did not kill his wife, and it is certain that she was poisoned, then who did kill her?'

'As to that, Inspector, it is for you to find out.'

Ghote retired to the sanctuary of Inspector Popatkar's office to consider his brush with Superintendent Chavan. He tried to envisage other possible people who might have wanted fifteen years before to have murdered the first Mrs Savarkar, but nothing but the vaguest and most unlikely of suppositions entered his head, ferret here and there among the papers on the case though he would.

In front of him Inspector Popatkar's chart of pickpocketing offences, with its graph-line curving steadily downwards, rebuked his own lack of success, and at last he jumped up from the small, file-cluttered desk determined at least to go and see the Swami again and gain himself some even more needed breathing-space.

But outside his door he found that all attempts to maintain an atmosphere of 'Business as usual' in the police-station had been abandoned. The constables were all wearing khaki-coloured steel helmets, looking a little ridiculous indoors but nevertheless unpleasant portents of what must be going on in the streets. The main doors of the building had been firmly locked and the windows of the outer office had had tall wooden shutters put up in front of them. Through these the noise of the crowd outside could be heard with ominous distinctness.

Ghote put an eye to one of the small holes that were bored in the centre of the shutters. Just a yard away from him he saw a great naked hair-covered chest. It was working in and out with the violence of the words it was rhythmically shouting.

But the 'Ghote go' the chant had started with had long ago been absorbed. And now the sound that battered on his ears was a meaningless, tirelessly repeated 'O ay o, o ay o.'

On and on it went.

O ay o. O ay o.

Ghote turned away from his spy-hole. He sought out the duty sergeant.

'I am going to leave by the back way,' he said. 'I am going to visit the Swami.'

The steady veteran sergeant considered gravely.

'It is certainly all right to go out at the back, Inspector,' he said. 'Those fools outside there are still content to be shouting only, so they are not thinking of going anywhere but in the street there. But it might be dangerous to show yourself near the Swami.'

'Do you think I will be recognized?' Ghote said, glancing down at his anonymous white shirt and trousers.

The sergeant took his time to think about it.

'Inspector, they are still looking for a man in uniform,' he said. 'From some of the shouts we heard before, when they had not started the chanting, we know that. So if you take that box you have, the one for the chicken-feed with the eggs in it, then you would be safer.'

'All right,' Ghote said wearily.

He was beginning to hate that box with a wild unreasoning hatred as if it was a stone roped round his neck.

'Inspector,' the sergeant called out after him as he began to go.

'Yes?'

'Are there real eggs in the box Perhaps if so it would be better to remove. You may have to undertake avoiding action.'

'No,' Ghote said with sudden stubbornness. 'If I have to take the box I take the whole box.'

The brightly-coloured box, however, seemed to bring him good luck. He had no difficulty in leaving the police-station compound and armed with clear directions he made his way easily towards the river through a network of narrow lanes. Comforting numbers of townspeople unaffected by the noise in the main street looked up at him with only mild curiosity. He passed a street of wheelwrights all busy thumping and banging at the gigantic heavy wooden wheels of the bullock carts and not at him. He threaded his way along a street of ropemakers, with the long half-finished ropes in process of being plaited constituting obstacles in plenty strung out as they were, but obstacles that had no evil intent about them.

And in due course he came out on to the river road at a point he recognized as being not far from the place where he had accosted by mistake the lonely Jain holy man. He was still there too, a softly meandering white figure beside the umbrella-like banyan under the grey rain-threatening sky. Ghote cycled past him, momentarily contrasting his ritual of non-violentness with the ritual hatred he had left behind in the main street.

Yet he too was engaged himself, he reflected, on an errand of violence. He was going to try to browbeat the Swami into silence by means of a piece of secret knowledge that he happened to have acquired.

He swung round the curve in the road that would reveal the ruined temple.

And jammed on the brakes of his battleship machine with a wet squeal.

There, spread all across the wide road in front of him, was another group of protesters, evidently coming away from the Swami in order to pour new zeal into the main demonstration in the town. And immediately it was obvious that the mood of this crowd was for the most part very different from that of the mob outside the police-station. Certainly the central bulk of the oncomers were making sounds full of sharp despair.

Ghote listened carefully for a moment or two.

Yes, they were not shouting 'Ghote go'. What were the words now?

He listened again.

He had them. 'Save our Swami. Save our Swami.' That was it.

And surely this meant that the Swami was failing. He might even be at the point of death. The crowd would turn into savages if he were to die.

Then he noticed that just to one side of the leaders of the straggling crowd there were three men who looked a little different from the others. They were all heavily-built and each carried a short, sturdy pole on which a piece of cardboard had been fixed bearing the old words 'Ghote Go'. The lettering was neat and bold, and to Ghote's quickly reacting imagination seemed to indicate an unlikely degree of organization. The men too, though not the goondas of the night before, looked far from being the idealistic sort of people who might be expected to be leading a protest march. They were walking along tight-lipped and without shouting. And they were looking keenly from side to side.

Had the Chairman sent them out to the temple to spearhead further protests? And had he given them an effective description of the man they were to chase from the town or to put out of action altogether?

He was unable to repress a hard tremble that moved up his body from calves to shoulders.

It was too late to retreat. That was certain. If he turned and fled he would draw the attention of everyone in that widespread crowd to himself. There was no one else near him, nothing else for them to look at.

And to one side there was the swollen mass of the river, a healthy gurgling yellow barrier. While on the far side of the road a steep bank made flight equally impracticable.

By now he had recovered a little from his initial shock and he realized there was only one thing to do. He would have to move very slowly and quietly out of the mob's way. Anything in the nature of a violent movement would inevitably draw the three goondas' particular notice.

Perhaps, of course, they were already discussing among themselves whether this figure on the bicycle was the one they were out to find.

Ghote dismounted and began pushing the ironclad machine towards the river side. He calculated that a plunge into water for a second time was his only slim chance of escaping if he had to. But the river looked as if it would be nothing like as easy to cross as the tank. It was flowing strongly as could be, and the thought of being swept along while a vengeful crowd kept pace with him on the bank was not one to be dwelt on.

Ten yards to go to the edge of the road.

Five.

He was there. And no arm had been extended pointing in his direction, no sharp cry of pursuit had superimposed itself over the almost plaintive shouting of 'Save our Swami'.

He slewed the bicycle round and stood still. Within a few moments one of the wings of the mob was passing him, a cluster of hangers-on by the looks of things, much less affected than most by the prevailing emotion. A youth in a checked shirt with a stubby knife brazenly stuck in his belt halted just in front of him.

'Are you coming to the police-station, bhai?' he demanded.

Ghote licked his lips.

'Sorry,' he said, 'I am on business today.'

'Business? Business?' the youth jeered. 'What business is more important than getting that wicked Ghote out of our town? Are you coming?'

'Well,' Ghote answered, 'perhaps I could catch you up when I have completed what I have to do. I have bicycle, you see.'

He patted the machine's broad saddle.

'Are you coming rightaway, or am I throwing that bicycle in the river?' the young man said.

Ghote thought fast. He had no doubt he could deal with an idle boaster like this easily enough on his own. But any scuffle might draw yet more attention to him.

'Are you coming?' the youth demanded again.

For a moment Ghote hesitated.

Then two youths, each also wearing a colourful shirt, started tugging at their companion's arms.

'Oh, come on,' the first of them said to him.

'Come on, or we shall be right at back for throwing stones at the police-wallas,' the other added.

The youth with the knife was in two minds. But abruptly the attraction of stone-throwing won.

'You wait till I come back,' he shouted threateningly at Ghote.

And then he hurried off after his friends.

Ghote waited where he was while the rest of the crowd marched by him. Then he quietly mounted his heavy bicycle and pedalled on till he came to the ruined temple once more.

There were many fewer people about than there had been on his first visit. Down among the crop of temporary shelter-like huts on the wide river strand there was scarcely a soul to be seen, merely two or three tattered and crouching old women sitting round a wisp of a fire. Ghote supposed that all the rest of the inhabitants of this camp – and it had grown larger than on his previous visit unless he was much mistaken – had gone, as particular devotees of the Swami, on this new march of protest over his declining condition.

For a moment he confronted the possibility of encountering them all if the Swami should die. And then resolutely he thrust the thought out of his head. The Swami's death would be an event so overwhelmingly appalling that it was not even to be considered.

Quickly Ghote got off the bicycle, pushed it out of sight behind the split and tortured trunk of an old pipal tree and clipped his chain and padlock round the rear wheel.

For an instant he looked at the egg-box on the carrier. The Swami had objected in no uncertain terms to his bringing it into the temple on his first visit, should he take it in now?

He decided that he would not. What he was going to say to the bad-tempered old holy man would cast him down enough. There was no need deliberately to annoy him as well.

He marched quickly over to the temple building. Inside it was nearly deserted, though not quite so. Certainly there were many fewer people than there had been last time. Only two beggars sat sprawled in the entrance, one of them with a huge swelled leg that must prevent him walking, the other with no legs at all, just two rag-wrapped stumps.

But at the gloomy back of the temple the alcove where the

Swami had sat before was empty. Only its army of differently-framed photographs, their renewed marigold garlands smelling pungently as ever, testified that this was a shrine.

Had he died then? Surely not. The old women, pottering about the building were subdued but not utterly downcast.

He cautiously explored the furthermost depths of the half-ruined hall. And at last he came upon a low archway right at the back. He peered round it.

He found a long, narrow room, lit only by a split in its stone walls through which there penetrated a greenish light, filtered by the pale leaves of the pipal trees all round the temple. In the room were two figures.

There was the Swami, sitting cross-legged almost exactly as he had been before in his alcove, and there was another man, the sight of whom caused Ghote's mouth to go suddenly dry with apprehension.

He was a doctor. No doubt about it. A stethoscope hung round his neck, its silvery end-piece glinting in the thick gloom. A Sikh, bushy-bearded and burly, he wore an open-necked dark blue shirt and dark trousers and a fine white turban bound on with surgical neatness.

A doctor. So it had come to that.

Ghote nerved himself up and went in. When he was half way across towards the Sikh he coughed, once and sharply.

The doctor swung round.

'Oh,' he said in sudden puzzlement. 'Who are you? You're not from the hospital?'

'You were expecting somebody from the hospital?' Ghote asked, his heart sinking further.

'The Medical Superintendent was to send some drugs I thought I might need, later on,' the Sikh said.

He frowned. Ghote could see his bushy eyebrows contract.

'But who are you then, if you're not from the hospital?' he asked.

'My name is Ghote.'

'Ghote – Good God, you're not the fellow . . . ?'

'Yes,' said Ghote, 'I am.'

The Sikh looked at him in silence for a second or two. Then he spoke.

'Better go over there. I don't want him unnecessarily disturbed.'

He jerked his head back at the motionless figure of the Swami.

They walked together back down the long darkened room to the doorway. There Ghote felt he could speak a little more loudly.

'His condition is serious then?' he asked.

The doctor looked at him speculatively.

'Well,' he replied at last, 'no point in sparing you the truth. Yes, his condition is bad. He could go at any time.'

He shrugged his broad shoulders beneath their blue shirt.

'On the other hand,' he said, 'he could last some while longer. It's a curious thing the will, you know. Something our medical science can never quite reckon with.'

'I have got to talk with him,' Ghote said.

'You have? He's my patient, you know. I don't think I'm going to let you.'

'He's your patient?' Ghote asked. 'What exactly does that mean?'

'Mean? Mean? I don't follow.'

'Put it this way. Whose doctor are you? Were you sent here by the Municipal Chairman?'

The Sikh grinned suddenly. White teeth splitting the curly black beard.

'Good lord, no,' he said. 'Dr Patil up at the hospital sent me, so far as anyone did. At first we looked in just every so often, though now someone's on duty all the time. It's me for the rest of today, and he's my boy.'

Ghote had found this brisk dismissal of the Chairman and his wide-flung nets reassuring.

'I will tell you what my trouble is,' he said.

'Your trouble, old man,' said the Sikh, 'is that if my patient dies you're going to get torn into little pieces.'

'I know that, but this is something different. You see, I have discovered that that old man there is the brother of the Chairman's father-in-law.'

The Sikh took a little time to take this in and consider its implications.

'I see that you would indeed want to talk with him,' he said at last. 'And since, I suppose, it will be the end of his fast, by all means go ahead. But take it easy, you know. Any violent shock might topple him over.'

Ghote looked at the free-and-easy figure beside him with some apprehension.

'But I shall nevertheless be administering something of a violent shock,' he said.

'Of course, old boy. And all I can say is good luck to you.'

The Sikh grinned broadly through his dark beard.

'You deserve it,' he said. 'The wicked old man.'

He offered him then to Ghote with a gesture of invitation.

Ghote went back down the long room till he was standing just in front of the unmoving Swami. He crouched down. Once again he was face to face with the old man.

He saw now that the beady eyes were wide open and might well be taking in the fact of who it was before him. He thought he saw too that the fast-purified flesh, visible in the small centre of that vast, gushing, ash-smeared beard, looked even more translucent than it had before.

He hardly dared speak.

'Do you know who I am?' he said at last.

'I told you to go,' came the fiercely irate voice he remembered.

He felt a little encouraged.

'But it was my duty to stay,' he replied. 'And I did stay. And while I stayed I learnt some facts. Facts, not about the man you are trying to protect – '

'He is not to have his peace broken,' the Swami suddenly burst in, a gush of blood seeming to come up into the soap-like pallor of his flesh.

'It is not about him that I learnt what I learnt,' Ghote went on after a few moments' pause. 'I regret to have to state that it is about you yourself.'

He looked intently at the grey jutting beard so close in front of him, and at the two eyes that burned steadily in the middle of it. But he saw no sign there of the dawning of what he had to say.

Implacably he went on.

'I learnt that you are the uncle of his wife,' he said.

He expected a reaction once the words had been said. None came.

He tried again. Perhaps the fasting old man could no longer take in everything that was said to him.

'I learnt that the Chairman you are trying to protect is your close relative, and that he came here in secret and begged you to save him from investigation.'

The beady eyes had taken it in. No doubt about that.

For a long time the still figure seated level with him said not a word. Then at last Ghote saw the answer coming, almost as if it was possible to observe its progress through the translucent flesh.

But it was not at all the answer he expected.

'Leave this town.'

He actually hopped back half a pace with the violence of the assault.

'You – You cannot continue your attempts to make me go when it will be known that you are the Municipal Chairman's uncle,' he said.

The eyes set in the middle of the gushing ash-plastered beard glowed fierily.

'I am telling you to go,' the Swami spat. 'I am telling you to get out. You are coming and interfering where you are not wanted, and you are to go.'

'I shall make it known about you and the Chairman,' Ghote threatened.

'I will protect my own family,' the Swami declared, poking his head furiously forward. 'I will protect him, and no one will lift their voice against me.'

'But why?' Ghote burst out. 'Why are you protecting him?'

'I protect him. Go from this town. I fast to death until you go.'

And those were the last words that Ghote was able to get out of him.

The interview petered to an end in a highly unsatisfactory way with Ghote, alternately standing and crouching, posing a series of more and more baffled questions and getting absolutely no answers, not so much as a sign of recognition. Eventually the

Sikh doctor, who had come up and was observing the scene with clinical interest, broke in.

'You might as well give up, old man,' he said. 'You won't get a word out of him any more, and I dare say I shall find the heart-beat rate gone all to hell.'

The possibility of seeing the Swami collapse lifeless at that very moment chilled Ghote like a plunge into an icy stream.

'I can see I must go,' he said.

'From the town?' the Sikh inquired cheerfully.

Ghote almost jumped off the floor with shock.

'Certainly not,' he replied. 'I have my duty to stay here and I will stay. There is still plenty for an investigating officer to in-quire into. The Chairman thinks he can banish every witness from the town. But we will see how well he can do it really.'

13

Before setting out in pursuit of the witness the Municipal Chairman had so cunningly attempted to put out of reach, Ghote returned to the besieged police-station.

If the Swami could not be persuaded to call off his campaign, he reasoned, then the least that could be done was to attempt to spread the facts about his relationship with the Chairman through the town and perhaps bite away at his influence in this manner. But he himself had no resources for rumour-spreading. To set a story going in the town he would have to go to the extent of telephoning the Eminent Figure in Bombay and waiting for him to telephone back to the small band of his supporters on the spot, a band which no doubt would grow like a swarm of bees if ever the Chairman were dislodged.

And the police-station was the only place from which Ghote could make a call. Humiliatingly, he lacked the money to do so from anywhere else.

But he found it harder to get back in than he had to get out. The newly-reinforced mob was not just yelling and shouting in the main street now. Bands and offshoots from it were roaming the lanes of the town everywhere, shouting slogans each according to its own particular convictions, or simply making mischief.

Several times he had to pedal his battleship-heavy bicycle for all he was worth in a direction that took him farther away from his objective in order to evade one or other of these bands. And on other occasions he had to skulk in a by-turning while noisy demonstrators went shouting by. Once even he had briefly to join one of the bands, dismounting from the bicycle and trudging along pushing it and shouting, without much enthusiasm, 'Ghote go, Ghote go.'

At last however he reached the mud-thick and ill-smelling lane at the rear of the police-station, only to be beset by new doubts.

What would his reception be here? Since he had left Superintendent Chavan, now unmasked as an open opponent, would have had plenty of time to poison the minds of every single constable in the station against him.

But apparently the superintendent's code of behaviour had ruled this out. The constable who answered his rattling at the narrow iron gate, the same man who had responded to his last call at the same place, was every bit as polite as before and within two minutes of wheeling the dreadnought bicycle into the safety of the compound Inspector Popatkar's office door was safely shut behind him.

And soon, with the shouting and fury from the main street just audible as a distant background to his thoughts, he was in touch first with a secretary in Bombay and then with the Eminent Figure himself.

In a jocular mood.

'Is that my mysterious correspondent that I am speaking with?'

'It is, sir,' Ghote replied, with a touch of sobering grimness.

'And have you sold a further quantity of feeding-stuff?'

'I think I may say so, sir. In fact – '

'Excellent, excellent,' the familiar precise voice interrupted. 'And I too have some profitable dealings to inform you of. You requested a check to be carried out for a certain missing receipt.

Well, I can report conclusively that neither that receipt nor the missing sample – the missing sample, you understand? – were ever received at this end.'

'Yes, sir, I understand,' Ghote replied, finding the enjoyment the Eminent Figure was so clearly deriving from his subterfuges more than he could easily take.

He was tempted to shout 'Organs, organs, the deceased's organs' down the line, which for once was extraordinarily clear. But he managed to hold himself in. Just.

'And you?' came the precise voice again. 'You have something to report also?'

'Yes, sir,' Ghote said cautiously.' I have to tell that I have learnt a certain fact with regard to the person-in-question. It concerns his relationship with a certain figure, a religious figure.'

He hoped that the excitement in the main street was distracting the operator in the exchange above the post office from his unofficial, though doubtless well-paid, listening duty.

'A religious figure? A religious figure? Inspector, what on earth are you talking of?'

Old fool.

'The inspection in question has been carried out, sir,' Ghote said, leaning heavily as an elephant on the word 'inspection'.

He quickly continued so as to give the Eminent Figure time to pull himself together.

'As to the second person, sir, he is the person causing a certain obstruction. You doubtless received reports of a campaign that was being mounted even before I arrived here, sir.'

He left it at that to see what reaction he got. The line was still beautifully clear and he felt he could almost hear the angry silence at the far end. But when at last the Eminent Figure spoke it was in quite a reasonable way.

'You have made a discovery, you say, about the relationship between this person and the main object of our inquiries?'

As neatly wrapped up as could be. He was learning, at last.

'Yes, sir,' Ghote said. 'A relationship of family, sir. They are closely connected.'

He took a quick breath and shot out the next words in a quick gabble.

'Brother of the deceased's father-in-law, sir.'

There was, clear to hear, a gasp of delight at the far end.

'Also, sir, our man made a personal and confidential request for the assistance.'

'He did, did he? Then I shall see that this gets known. It will be the end of all opposition to you.'

'I am afraid that is not necessarily so, sir. I have already put the facts before the certain figure and he has refused to alter his attitude.'

'He will do so once it is generally known. Mark my words.'

'Yes sir. Yet I have a feeling he will not be too much censured for supporting a member of his family only, sir.'

'Nonsense. What nonsense.'

The querulous voice positively spat along the line.

'Nonsense, man,' it repeated. 'Once it is known that all this objection has been purely a disgraceful instance of nepotism then everyone will turn against it.'

Ghote looked at the bright cardboard egg-container resting on Inspector Popatkar's desk.

'I hope it may be as you say, sir,' he replied. 'But in any case I assure you I shall remain here.'

'You are most certainly to stay,' the over-particular voice said firmly. 'If a murder has been committed you are to put the man responsible behind bars.'

Ghote thought of the likely listening ears at the exchange.

'Yes, sir. The line is murder,' he said quickly. 'These telephone-wallas should be put behind bars, I most certainly agree.'

It calmed the old man wonderfully.

'Yes, yes,' he said. 'As I was saying the line is murder. Yes. You are quite right, Inspe – you are quite right.'

'Sir,' Ghote put in, 'have you been able to act on the other matters I requested when I spoke to you last?'

'Oh yes, yes,' the thin voice said, still apologetic. 'I have put them all in hand. I have insisted on the utmost urgency. You need have no fears over that. But you yourself, my good sir, have you made any other progress?'

He had not, Ghote reflected. All he had done since he had last reported, was to have suffered under the Chairman's wiles, first escaping with his life from goondas, second finding that his one ally in the town was a spy.

'Most satisfactory progress, sir,' he nevertheless forced himself to reply, 'though I have no more new facts for you as of today.'

'Well,' said the faint voice, recovering some of its querulousness now, 'I trust I do not have to remind you that time is perhaps against you?'

'I know it, sir,' Ghote replied grimly. 'But kindly remember also that there are still steps to be taken at your end. There is the inquiry in a certain distant part of the country.'

'What distant part of the country? What is this? Are you still there?'

Silly old fool.

Ghote snapped the word out in one quick blip.

'Nagaland.'

'What did you – Oh, yes. Yes. That. Yes, I assure you that is being pressed as hard as all the other matters.'

'Then I will say good-bye, sir. And we will see what effect your other calls here may have.'

'They will do wonders, I promise.'

'We shall see, sir.'

And Ghote laid down the receiver.

He sat for some little time staring at the chart labelled 'Pickpocketing Offences' though without seeing it. His mind was busy thinking over the last few minutes.

The Eminent Figure might be only a mere irritation on the far end of the telephone, but if things went unsatisfactorily here in the end he could become a potent bringer of wrath back in Bombay.

Ghote felt suddenly hot to melting point.

Yet such a lot depended on what was done in Bombay. Alone in this town he himself might be able to achieve little, but he had the enormous advantage of having at call powerful assistance which could if necessary stretch all over India, to Nagaland where perhaps the missing pathologist might be found, to the highest and lowest reaches of Bombay where bit by bit enough evidence to bring a case might yet be assembled.

If only the Eminent Figure would act like a conscientious policeman.

Ghote jumped up determined that, whatever shortcomings his illustrious collaborator might betray, he himself would not let anything go by default here in the town for lack of thrustful investigation. He would go to that buxom liar Mrs Dhulup in the dhobis' quarter and force the truth about her husband's whereabouts from her.

But his vigour was to be checked like a damned river.

The police-station had been surrounded.

Setting out for the compound with his protective egg-box held in front of him, he had hardly bothered to think about the method of his departure. And then he found the high back wall of the compound lined by half a dozen lathi-armed constables scuttling about beating at the heads of lively figures popping up at different points. One of these he thought he recognized, indeed, his old acquaintance of the checked shirt and belt-stuffed knife who had actually succeeded in heaving himself chest-high across the top of the wall before a pair of constables at either side sent him squirming back with a rain of lathi blows. A heavy shower of stones from the far side of the wall followed this discomfiture.

So there was nothing for it but to spend champing hours in the station waiting for a chance to sneak out somewhere.

It came, in the end, quite suddenly. The skirmishing over the back wall seemed to have reached a steady pitch when a loud shouting voice was heard on the far side and abruptly the attackers up on the wall dropped down. They did not reappear.

After four or five minutes, during which the sounds of activity on the far side had gradually died right away, Ghote cautiously heaved himself up and put his head over the wall. The attackers had disappeared, every one. Indeed the sole human being to be seen was an old woman crouching not far from the corner of the compound, perhaps hoping to find something useful to her in the debris of the battle.

So, Ghote thought, a certain telephone call from Bombay has been made to certain unnamed individuals in the town and certain news is spreading.

He felt reassured and called out a cheerful bulletin to the constables waiting below leaning on their lathis.

'I will be going now,' he ended.

His bicycle was quickly brought by one constable while another, somewhat reverently, carried out the egg-box. He received first the dreadnought machine and then the box, thanked the constables and prepared to set off.

Already it was getting on towards evening. Crows were flapping their way homeward under a sky of huge slowly moving grey clouds. Their cawing seemed to be the only sound to be heard.

There was no time now to be lost. He swung his foot over the crossbar of the ponderous cycle.

'Inspector Ghote. Inspector Ghote.'

In the very act of putting his foot on the bicycle's far upraised pedal he halted, frozen.

His name. Shouted after him. When he had already assumed his disguise. Known.

He twisted round.

It must have been the old scavenging woman who had called out to him. Had she been left by the rioters as a spy?

She was coming towards him now, hobbling and bent. He looked at her carefully.

She was carrying something, a glinting pot-shaped object, which it was difficult to make out clearly in the poor light.

Then, with a sudden little start of recognition, he knew who the old crone was. The pot-shaped object was a huge Ovax jar. It was the aged harijan woman he had tripped over in his first moments in the town, when he had so nearly broken his eggs and had seen that disturbing copy of *Time* magazine.

How on earth had she discovered his name? Had something during their brief encounter three days ago betrayed him? It could not have done.

He saw the scimitar-nosed, hair-decorated face he remembered looking up at him.

'I must see Inspector Ghote. He is in police-station?'

He hardly realized in his agitation what the import of the old crone's words were. Then it came to him. She did not know who she was talking to.

'I have no time, no time to be answering questions,' he shouted at her.

And he forcibly jerked the ironclad bicycle upright, leant his full weight on one pedal and with a fearful swerve right across the whole width of the narrow lane he shot off into the dark greyness of the late day.

As he headed at a great rate towards the river and the dhobis' quarter, it began to rain again, though not very hard. Evidently this put a final end to any demonstrating for the time being. The only people he saw on the whole ride were honest citizens hurrying about their business under beetle-like black umbrellas.

Ram Dhulup's wife was not this time seated outside her small house, but she was just inside the open door, sitting there on a mat looking dreamy and far-away with a more colourful sari on even than at his first visit and smelling strongly of Queen of the Night scent.

Ghote did not need to ask her whether her husband had returned. Plainly she was expecting some other visitor.

'Well,' he said, violently interrupting her reverie, 'let me tell you straightaway that I am a policeman. An inspector, CID.'

To his delight he obtained an immediate response to this slapped-down threat, a look of sudden blankly uncomprehending fear. Plainly whatever had been said to the girl by the Chairman's henchmen in the spiriting away of Ram Dhulup had not been enough. She had been taught how to be a little insolent to anybody making inquiries and she had been told she could give them the false address in Nagpur, but she had not been strengthened against really pointed questioning.

Ghote stood over her now, legs apart, blocking the low entrance to the mud-walled house.

'Yes,' he said, 'an inspector of the CID, and you have told me lies, isn't it?'

'No, no.'

But the denial was so obviously offered as a mere hurriedly snatched up shield that it positively constituted an open admission.

'Yes,' Ghote said, remorselessly putting on the pressure, 'you have told me lies. You have told that your husband is in Nagpur. He is not. Where is he?'

'I do not – He is in Nagpur, yes.'

She began feebly bleating out the fictitious address once more, as if it were some sort of charm that might protect her from this assault.

'Stop that,' Ghote snapped. 'Nagpur was cut off by floods at the time you said your husband was making the journey. Do you think police inspectors are absolute fools?'

'No. No. I do not know.'

In the darkness caused by his body blocking the doorway Ghote could see the girl's large nose-jewel flashing and bobbing in her agitation.

'You know very well where is your husband,' he thundered. 'And you are going to tell me. Now.'

'I do not know. I cannot say.'

'You know and you will say.'

Something inside her, some untapped well of strength, gave her a sharp access of strength. He saw her teeth flash once more in an insolent smile and prepared himself for an impudent answer.

It would do her no good, he thought. She was the sort to break sooner or later. The only doubt was whether in fact she really did know more than that some followers of the Chairman had come and whisked the inconvenient Ram Dhulup away and had fed her with a few lies to tell any questioners. However he would find out soon enough. In the meanwhile let her have her moment of impudence.

The kohl-darkened eyes glinted up at him.

'He is gone to Nagpur,' she said. 'Do you think there is one way only of going? If the railway is cut then he can go on foot. You think because many years ago his feet were cut off he cannot walk? I tell you he can go faster than you can, Mr Inspector.'

Ghote swung right round in the low doorway and left her. After all, he reflected, what need to bully if he had accidentally just learnt more than the girl probably knew herself?

14

Ghote almost rushed off there and then to act on the discovery he had made. His mind bubbled with ideas.

If the crippled servant he had glimpsed at his last visit to the Municipal Chairman's house, scuttling away from the gates on a pair of wildly swinging crutches, really was Ram Dhulup – and the more he thought about it the more he was convinced, for why else but as a method of concealment would the Chairman employ such a cripple? – then the problem ahead was somehow to get inside the Chairman's compound to talk with the missing dhobi.

Or to get Ram Dhulup out.

But both courses presented considerable difficulties. The Chairman's house was very much of a fortress. There was that high wall surrounding the whole compound and topped with barbed wire. There was the fact that in its whole length, as he had learnt from young Vasant, there was only the one pair of gates and that these were always kept closed. And there was the tall chaprassi who guarded these gates, and doubtless a fair number of other toughs always at hand.

Reluctantly Ghote in the end postponed any attempt to take advantage of his lucky discovery until the next day. Other people's watchmen slept, but he doubted very much whether the Chairman's did.

He propelled the battleship bicycle along to the railway station and there once more occupied an illegal bed.

But he set off in the morning – the sixty-fourth day of the Swami's fast, he told himself as he woke – while the light was still coming up in the sky and zoomed his weighty bicycle along towards the town and through it busy considering the details of a plan that had planted itself in his head during the night.

There was nobody in sight as, at the same kika-thorn patch where he had learnt from Vasant about the relationship between the Swami and the Chairman, he dismounted and concealed his machine. There was no one around to see him and quite soon he was able to get up right to the sloping irregular mud-plastered wall at the back of the compound and listen to the sounds of the extensive household inside beginning its day. Before long he had located, he hoped, the part of the wall that gave on to the servants' quarter. He hurried back to his bicycle and from the little leather pouch that hung from the back of the saddle he extracted the larger of the two tyre-levers it contained. It was only a small strip of metal, four or five inches long, but he thought it would serve his purpose.

He took it back to his chosen spot on the high wall and began to hollow out two toe-holds for himself in the impacted mud. When he was certain they were deep enough to give him the little extra support he calculated he would need on the slightly sloping surface of the wall, he put the lever in his pocket, stepped back a few paces, took a quick run up and jumped.

His fingers found the broad tiled top to the wall and a moment later his scrabbling left foot struck against one of his newly-made toe-holds. He dug this foot in, fished round with the other foot until he had located the companion hold and felt himself to be safe. Then he ventured to peer over the wall.

The servants' quarter, a row of hut-like dwellings, lay just underneath his eye.

Now to see whether Ram Dhulup would come within call, and would come alone.

He spotted him within two minutes of his watch beginning. But, in spite of the former dhobi having no apparent duties in the household, he did not seem ever to be alone. First he had stopped to chat with one of the elderly women servants from the house, and, to Ghote's fury, even when she kept telling him that she ought to get back inside or things would start to go wrong, he persisted in talking to her. And it was not as if his conversation was about anything either. It was all too plain that he had nothing to do and was badly bored.

When at last he was deserted by the elderly servant, at once he started off to look for someone new to talk to. This time he settled on one of the malis, already beginning work breaking up the earth in a rain-flattened flowerbed. And now he was well into the middle of the compound, too far to call to even if the gardener left him.

It looked as if he would have spent the whole morning there too, only a shower of rain began. Ghote felt the first heavy drops striking on his shoulders as he lay spreadeagled on the high wall. But even though they penetrated his shirt straight away he was not put out: surely the fellow would make his way back to the shelter of the huts now, and if he did so . . .

And, like a clockwork show, it suddenly all began to fall out exactly to the pattern Ghote had envisaged.

The rain started to come down more heavily. Ram Dhulup looked up at the sky and then reluctantly began swinging his way on his crutches over towards the shelter of the huts. Simultaneously everybody else who had been outside got themselves in and so within a minute there was no one about at all. And the crippled dhobi, though feeling obliged to take cover from the downpour, evidently was still determined to keep a look-out for possible company. So he stayed only just inside the doorway of the hut he had entered.

Ghote let a further two minutes go slowly by – the shirt was clamped to his back now by the force of the raindrops – and then he took his courage in his hands and softly called out.

'Ram Dhulup. Ram Dhulup.'

But the slapping patter of the rain prevented the quiet sound reaching the footless cripple.

'Ram Dhulup,' Ghote called now more urgently.

And then the former dhobi looked up.

He looked all round him unable to make out where this unfamiliar voice calling his name had come from.

'Here, Ram Dhulup, here,' Ghote called down.

The man began to look quite frightened, as if he was being summoned by a heavenly avenger to be called to account for his misdeeds.

'Here, you fool, here. Up on the wall.'

At last the cripple's darting gaze fixed on him.

'Come here,' Ghote commanded sharply. 'I have something to tell you.'

The cripple looked all round him to make sure nobody was

watching. It was evident he had been instructed he was on no account to give away to any outsider his presence concealed inside the Chairman's large and well-walled compound.

'Ram Dhulup,' Ghote called, as the man still hesitated, 'I have something to tell you about your wife.'

The cripple gave a last quick look round, in such a panic that he was not really seeing anything, and then swinging his crutches mightily he came swooping over to the wall.

'What is it? What is it?' he demanded, his face a map of half-realized and rejected fears.

'I came specially to speak with you,' Ghote said, looking down at the lined face of the cripple under a not altogether clean white head-cloth.

He knew he had his man hooked now. He could afford to speak quietly and to play him.

'I considered it my duty to come,' he added.

'Yes, yes. But what is it? What has she done?'

'I cannot tell such things over a wall,' Ghote answered with a calmness he calculated to be maddening.

The cripple cast a fearful glance all round him.

'But I cannot come out,' he said.

'You must.'

'But tell, tell me only, who is it?'

'I cannot say a word when I am up here like this. Will you meet me outside?'

'I am not allowed to go.'

'But when you have urgent private business. What is this "not allowed"?'

The cripple plainly resented this. His well-developed shoulders writhed over his crutches.

'Who are you?' he demanded abruptly. 'I have never seen – '

Ghote silenced him with one furious 'Shush'.

'Someone coming,' he lied in a ferocious whisper. 'Meet me in among the first kika thorns on the road into town. Quickly, before it is too late.'

He let himself slide down the wet and slippery surface of the wall and landed with a small squelch at the bottom.

As far as he could judge he had surely got his man, yet it was not without anxiety that he returned at a crouching run to where his bicycle lay hidden. But it was important to get Ram Dhulup right outside the Chairman's power. He was never going to tell what he had to tell when at any moment some loyal follower of his boss might spot him.

Cautiously thrusting his way underneath the devilishly sharp thorn bushes, their fan-like leaves catching the rain and directing it all down, it seemed, on to his already soaked garments, he heaved and pushed himself to a point where he could watch the road and remain unseen.

Would Ram Dhulup succeed in wheedling or tricking his way past the chaprassi at the Chairman's gates? In all probability the fellow had orders not to let this particular dependent out in any circumstances. How would he keep to them?

On the muddy, puddled surfaces of the road the raindrops splashed ploppingly. Ghote strained to see as far along towards the houses as he could. But raising himself more than an inch or two off the ground sent a network of thorns prickling bloodily into his unprotected back and he had to flop back and content himself with a limited field of vision.

And then, above the irregular splashing rhythm of the rain, he detected another splashing rhythm, heavier and perfectly regular. It was the cripple's crutches, making frantic haste along the squelchy road.

Victory.

Ghote wriggled downwards out of the thorn patch, his small sense of triumph jerking out of him with every new twist and scrape of his body. All right, so he had persuaded the fellow out of the Chairman's power, but would it have all been in vain? How much would he prove to know about what had gone on at those Coroner's Committee meetings fifteen years ago?

Ram Dhulup appeared at the edge of the road, looking down over the kika thorns in a state of evident anxiety.

'This way,' Ghote called.

Manoeuvring himself with remarkable dexterity, the cripple made his way down along the narrow path that Ghote himself had taken when he had come to meet Vasant. One thing was certain: his luscious young wife had not been lying when she had said that his crutches hardly interfered with his progress.

And in less than a minute Ram Dhulup was tossing the crutches down on to the wet ground and was crouching on his footless stumps waiting to hear what Ghote had to tell him.

'My wife,' he said, 'what is it that you know?'

'I have seen your wife since you have been kept hidden at the Chairman's house,' Ghote answered ambiguously. 'On two days I have seen her.'

'Yes, yes. And what was it that she was doing? Who was there with her?'

Stuffing his implied confirmation that Ram Dhulup had been kept out of the way by the Chairman into a safe place in the corner of his mind, Ghote released one more driblet of information.

'Yesterday I saw her towards evening,' he said. 'You know a green sari she has with blue circles on?'

'The one with the gold border,' Ram Dhulup said, as if this alone confirmed his worst fears.

'Yes, it had gold border. And now I want you to tell me some things I need badly to know.'

'But was there someone there in the house also?' Ram Dhulup demanded.

'I will tell you everything I saw,' Ghote said. 'But later. First you must tell me what I want to know.'

'What do you want to know? What do you want to know about? Who are you?'

'I am a police officer. My name is Ghote.'

In the shadow of the thorn brake Ghote saw Ram Dhulup's face go suddenly taut. The cripple cast around urgently for his crutches and seemed as if he was going to heave himself to his feet there and then and make off as fast as he could.

'Stop,' Ghote snapped out. 'You wish to hear what I saw of your wife?'

Ram Dhulup was caught by the words literally off-balance. His right hand swayed as he scrabbled round on the damp earth for one of the crutches and he kept his eyes imploringly fixed on Ghote's.

'But – But if – But they would kill me,' he said at last.

'Who would kill you?' Ghote demanded.

'The goondas. The Chairman's goondas. I have seen them. They came in secret to the house two days ago, very early in the morning. I only was awake. I could not sleep. I had such dreams about – '

Ram Dhulup stopped abruptly. His eyes left Ghote's and he looked down shamefacedly at the ground beside his stump legs.

'Such dreams about my wife,' he whispered.

'And you saw the Chairman talking with these goondas?' Ghote asked. 'You knew that they were goondas?'

'Yes, yes. I heard a little also. From that I was able to tell what manner of men they were. There was talk of putting someone out of the way, and they agreed to it.'

'You did not hear who this person was?' Ghote asked.

'No. But I heard the Chairman ask them to do that, and I saw by the looks of the men that they would do it. I cannot stay here. I cannot stay one more second.'

Ram Dhulup actually took his eyes from Ghote's face and found one heavy crutch where it lay on the soft ground.

'Wait,' Ghote said with calmness. 'Shall I tell who that man was whose death was being ordered? It was me. And look, am I dead? Am I hurt even?'

Slowly Ram Dhulup's fingers released the crutch and it dropped again to the sodden earth.

'It was you?' he whispered.

'Yes, it was me. You see, nobody is as powerful as they would like people to believe.'

Ram Dhulup took it in.

'And now,' Ghote said briskly, 'think about your life as it was fifteen years ago.'

'Fifteen years ago?'

For a moment Ram Dhulup was puzzled.

'It is fifteen years and a little since the accident,' he said wonderingly. 'When my first wife was killed, and I also nearly. When I lost the feet of both legs.'

He looked down at his rag-protected stumps.

'And it is fifteen years also,' Ghote put in, 'since you were a member, one of five, of a certain Coroner's Committee.'

'No,' said Ram Dhulup aghast. 'Not that.'

'Come,' Ghote answered. 'That is why you were taken from your home three days ago, is it not? Of course I am wanting to know about that time.'

Ram Dhulup was silent. He darted a glance over his shoulder into the thorn brake as if he feared that even in its depths someone would be crouching listening.

'Now,' Ghote said briskly, 'how was it that you came to be on that committee? You were a dhobi then, or, worse, a dhobi who had just lost both feet in an accident. Why were you chosen?'

'I do not know, sahib.'

'You know.'

'Sahib, it was because I had lost my feet, because I was poor. He knew I needed money most of all.'

'Who knew?'

'He, sahib. The Chairman.'

It was a whisper of admission.

Ram Dhulup looked up into Ghote's face now it was made.

'Sahib,' he said more courageously, 'in those days he was not Chairman. It was his father-in-law, the man who was to become his father-in-law who was Chairman.'

'Yes, I know.'

'So it was just Vinayak Savarkar who came to me.'

'He came himself?'

'Sahib, this was matter in which one does not trust even one's closest friends.'

'I see. So he came to you himself, in secret? And what did he ask of you?'

'Yes, sahib, it was in secret. And he asked me first just to be on this what-they-call committee. And to tell everything to him that was said. And then to be ready, sahib.'

'Ready for what?'

'To do whatever he said, sahib.'

'I see. And were you in the end asked to do anything?'

'Oh yes, sahib.'

'And what was that?'

'It was when we had heard much talk already about the lady who was dead.'

'What was it he asked?'

'I was to say something, sahib. Without fail I was to say.'

'And what was it?'

'I was to say that because he was a good Brahmin and she also – But, sahib, he was not good Brahmin. Everyone knew. I also knew. I had seen him with my own eyes do such things. Outcaste people he would touch even, sahib.'

'But what was it you were asked to do?' Ghote hammered.

'To say that, sahib. That he was good Brahmin and the dead lady also. To say how terrible it would be that she should not go to the burning ghats, sahib.'

'Go on, go on.'

'Well, this I did, sahib. All that he told me. I said he was good Brahmin, though, sahib, sometimes since I have wondered at what his parents must have been. Such things he does, sahib, such things he dares to do. What did they ever teach him as child?'

'And you suggested that the body should after all be burned?' Ghote prompted. 'And what happened?'

'It was agreed, sahib. It was agreed that in one month it could be taken from the earth and burned.'

'I see.'

'And that was done too, sahib. I was there. I helped, as if I had been brother to her. There was no one else who knew, and who was allowed.'

Then suddenly, appalled at the extent of his betrayal of his patron, Ram Dhulup positively grabbed his two thick crutches and thrusting their ends into the squelchy ground heaved himself to his feet.

Ghote calculated rapidly. He could try and force the man to stay and then squeeze more details out of him about just what had gone on in the Coroner's Committee. But keeping him here increased second by second the chances of his being caught by someone from the Chairman's house.

He rose to his feet as well.

'How did you get past the chaprassi?' he asked Ram Dhulup.

'Sahib, it cost me much money. But sahib I must know. My wife, who was she with?'

Ghote came to an abrupt decision.

'Yes,' he said, 'your wife was wearing that green and blue sari with the gold border last night. But there was no one with her and I said such things to her that she will dare have no one.'

Ram Dhulup seized his hand in his own, made horny by the long use of his crutches. But Ghote shook himself free.

'Now,' he said, 'quickly, get back to the house. Let no one know you were here. The chaprassi will dare say nothing with you there to see he keeps his word. Go now.'

And like a flapping horn-winged creature the cripple hoisted himself at top speed up the narrow path to the roadway and away along the puddle-splotched surface of the road in the direction of the Municipal Chairman's house.

Ghote stood where he was in the shelter of the kika brake and blew a long sigh. He was soaking wet. His shirt and trousers, clean and white only a couple of hours earlier, were mud-smeared from head to foot with his vigil on the wall and his spying under the thorn bushes. But he was content.

There could be no doubt now that the Chairman had gone to extraordinary lengths to make sure that Coroner's Committee did just what he wanted. He had virtually seen to it himself that his dead wife's body was taken to the burning ghats instead of being buried and subject to exhumation. All right, doubtless Superintendent Chavan would say that this was simply because someone unknown had poisoned her and the Chairman feared to have suspicion cast on him, but it could equally be that it was because he had poisoned her himself. It was in fact much more likely.

Certainly this discovery meant he had taken another good step on the road to getting an ultimate conviction. And there would be other steps to come, steps freed from even the least shadow of doubt.

15

So it was at a decidedly swift pace that Inspector Ghote approached the town police-station again that morning. It was becoming more and more urgent to get from the Eminent Figure in Bombay the answers to the various questions he had put to him, and especially he wanted a reply to the inquiries that were being made, he hoped, in Nagaland about the whereabouts of Hemu Adhikari, the pathologist who had actually handled the body of the Municipal Chairman's first wife, who had failed to dispatch the organs he had removed to the Chemical Examiner in Bombay and who so soon after undertaking that routine autopsy (in which the routine had mysteriously gone astray) had been firmly posted away to distant Nagaland. With cast-iron confirmation that the Chairman himself had made sure his poisoned wife's body was burned at the ghats, it became more than ever crucial to find out what had happened to the missing organs and how exactly they had been disposed of, if indeed they had been disposed of.

Another telephone call to Bombay was urgent.

He brought his dreadnought bicycle to a skiddy halt in the smelly lane at the back of the police compound, dismounted, leant the machine against the wall and began unstrapping the brightly-lettered egg-box before rattling for admittance on the narrow old rusty gate.

'Inspector Ghote.'

It was a lisping toothless voice from behind him.

He turned. The hair-sprouting crone he had first encountered as he had arrived in the town was standing there again, still clutching her huge Ovax jar of pathetic possessions. In his hurry to get to Ram Dhulup's house when the rioting had died down the evening before and in the excitement of finding out just where the Chairman had hidden the missing dhobi he had totally forgotten his curious meeting with her at this very spot then.

Why had she wanted to see the Inspector Ghote she did not know she had already actually met?

Well, he had no time to find out now.

He took the egg-box off the bicycle carrier, tucked it under his arm and gave the iron gate a rattle.

'Inspector Ghote it is you,' the old woman mumbled at him through toothless gums.

So she had found out. Damn.

'Yes, yes,' he answered, 'I am Inspector Ghote, but I have no time to be talking now. If you have business with me you should tell to the constables round at the front, they will say when I can talk, if I can talk at all.'

He saw now with pleasure that a constable was coming across the compound at a smart double. Superintendent Chavan may have let him down, but there was no doubt he knew how to run an efficient force.

'Inspector Ghote,' the old woman lisped out again, seeming almost content simply to be repeating this magic name.

The constable unlocked the gate, came out and seized the bicycle's handlebars with eagerness. Ghote stepped smartly towards the gate after him. The old woman put a tentative, talon-nailed hand on to his sleeve. Almost without having to make any conscious effort he pulled his arm from the feeble grasp and entered the compound. There apparently the old crone did not dare follow him. He turned his head to shout to her again to go around and tell the desk what her business was, but abandoned the attempt before he had begun it. There was no time to waste in an effort destined from the start to be abortive.

Inside, in Inspector Popatkar's office he eagerly picked up the telephone receiver and gave the magic sequence of the Bombay number.

Delays of every sort harassed his call this time. He was left for nearly ten minutes by the operator listening to two different intermingling tiny faraway conversations, one in Hindi about a new-born child, and the other in Gujarati about a fatal traffic accident in Bombay. Then, when abruptly his connection was made, it was as abruptly cut the moment the far end had spoken the number. He set to to obtain the connection again and was put through quickly this time, only it was to a number which turned out after a prolonged misunderstanding to be none other than that of the Palace Talkies. It took more than a quarter of an hour to disentangle the consequences of that.

And then finally when he did get through to the Bombay number and succeeded in asking for the Eminent Figure without suddenly being clicked into utter silence, the line he had been given proved to have some defect in it which meant that the voices at the far end were fainter if anything than the voices he had heard earlier excitedly discussing a birth and a death.

'Is that you, sir?' he bellowed.

'Yes, yes, it is me. Speak louder, if you please,' the Eminent Figure, though querulous as ever, bellowed back.

'Have you had results of inquiries in distant parts?' Ghote counter-bellowed, shouting each word separately and convinced that in all the time he had been trying to put the call through there had been ample opportunity for one of the Chairman's men to have been set to listen.

'In distant parts?' came the predictably querulous answer.

'Nagaland,' Ghote said in one quick shout.

'I cannot hear. You are extremely faint.'

And suddenly another voice, deafeningly loud to Ghote's ears, broke in.

'He is saying "Nagaland", caller.'

It was the operator, all eagerness to he helpful.

'Yes,' said Ghote wearily, 'Nagaland.'

'Certainly I have had results from Nagaland,' the faint, faint querulous voice said next.

Ghote's spirits shot up.

'What have you heard?' he almost demanded.

'The results have only just come to me,' the Eminent Figure said with a complacency which the tininess of his voice did not conceal.

Just, indeed. Most likely twelve hours ago, Ghote thought boilingly.

'I am completely satisfied with their thoroughness,' the Eminent Figure added.

'And you found?' Ghote yelled.

'The person in question became a hopeless addict of alcoholic liquor within three years of his arrival there,' the Eminent Figure shouted censoriously. 'He was well remembered by many people whom the person conducting my inquiry spoke with. But, although the man remained in the area for a considerable time, a virtual wreck of a creature, it is five years now at least since he was seen.'

'You are hearing, caller?' asked the operator in his cheerful voice of a thousand thunders.

'I am hearing.'

'In the circumstances,' came the faint voice of the Eminent Figure again, 'I think you can presume the fellow is dead. I have too often spoken of the ills excessive consumption of alcohol brings in its train – '

'And the other inquiries?' Ghote shouted out, feeling that the appalling line at least gave him the opportunity of cutting into a lecture.

'Other inquiries?'

'Bombay caller, he is asking about "other inquiries".'

'You mean the inquiries you asked me to have made here in Bombay?'

'He means – '

'I have heard,' Ghote screeched. 'And yes, I do mean those inquiries.'

'There have been delays and delays,' the tiny querulous voice said. 'But I am hopeful that quite soon we shall have something for you. And in the meanwhile what progress are you making at your end?'

Ghote leant back from the telephone and deliberately banged his palm violently down on the rest. If the Eminent Figure decided they had been cut off while he still had something worthwhile to say he could put in a fresh call himself.

In the meantime he had better things to do. Something was tickling in his mind. It had begun while the Eminent Figure was launching into his lecture on the evils of alcohol. Something in the way he had said that Hemu Adhikari must be dead had triggered off recollections of the manner in which the pathologist's old schoolmaster father had expressed the same idea.

The very words came, by an effort of will, back into his mind now. 'There is no Mr Adhikari Junior.' Had that been it? And 'I had a son: he no longer . . . ' It was 'no longer' something. 'No longer is in this world' or 'No longer exists.' More or less that. In any case whatever the exact form of the words there had been something curious about them. That much he was certain of.

Suddenly he jumped up from Inspector Popatkar's hard chair.

That was it. The upright old man's words had been just those of someone who made it a practice never to tell a lie and who yet wanted, for important and urgent reasons, for once to conceal the truth.

To conceal the truth. Then there was a truth to be concealed about the pathologist. And since what everybody was being led to believe was that he was dead, the truth could only be that he was alive.

Ghote ran down the passage and out to the bicycle rack in the compound. Half-way to the iron gate he realized he had forgotten his egg-box, but this was no time to go back for it.

Pedalling through the town at a fearful rate, swerving round puddles, sending scavenging chickens scuttling and squawking, attracting various barking pi-dogs to yelp at his heels for as long as their breath lasted, sweating like a waterworks in the damply humid air but happy that at least the rains with their way of blotting out all possibility of progress seemed to be slackening off, Ghote at last came to the sedate district of minor officials' homes where the little old upright ex-schoolmaster, Mr Adhikari, lived.

His house kept the same tranquil air as it had on his first visit. The long front wall was as neatly blank, the narrow front door as tightly closed as ever. Even the same wreck of a beggar slept propped up against the wall as he had slept before, lacking even the vigour to pursue his essentially unvigorous profession.

Yet, Ghote observed automatically as he got off the bicycle, here was a slight change. The man today was much nearer the house door than he had been before. Indeed he was so close to it that in one direction he would prevent anyone going straight up to it. Would the severe old schoolmaster fly into a rage when he opened the door and discovered him there?

Ghote propped the bicycle against the wall on the opposite side of the door. It seemed that the slight scraping clatter he made had disturbed the old wreck's sleep. He stirred and muttered a few barely decipherable words.

Ghote, with his hand raised to knock on the front door, stopped abruptly.

Egg-white. He thought he had heard the old beggar muttering something about egg-white of all things.

He shrugged.

He must have got eggs on the brain. Thank goodness, at least he had not got that confounded box with him now.

He knocked briskly at the door.

It opened almost at once. Little Mr Adhikari also looked exactly as he had done on the previous occasion. Again he wore only a white dhoti and again its pleats fell with wonderful neatness from his thin waist. Again his gold-rimmed pince-nez rested squarely and severely across the bridge of his nose.

He gave the slumped beggar a single swiftly suspicious glance but reserved his full attention for Ghote.

'Good morning,' Ghote said to him quickly. 'I have come to talk about your son.'

The little old man perceptibly stiffened.

'You have done that already,' he said. 'I have no more to tell.'

'You told that he no longer exists,' Ghote answered, ignoring the old schoolmaster's sharpness.

'Yes, yes, that is what I said.'

The little old man made as if to close the door.

'But what exactly did you mean by those words?' Ghote asked.

'I meant what I meant. And I have no time to be all the day talking.'

'Sir, I must remind you I am police officer. I am not talking only. I am investigating.'

'Then you choose a most extraordinary way of carrying out your duties,' Mr Adhikari retorted sternly.

'Sir, you choose a somewhat extraordinary form of expression to talk about your son.'

'What is it to you what form of words I use, if you please?'

'I am anxious only to know exactly what you were meaning.'

Little Mr Adhikari glared up at him furiously through his gold-rimmed spectacles.

'Young man,' he said, 'my meaning was perfectly clear.'

'Did you mean that your son is dead?' Ghote asked plainly.

For an instant the old man looked trapped, and Ghote felt positively sorry for him. But it was an instant only.

'What has come over the police force nowadays I cannot think,' the old man resumed almost at once. 'In my young days under the British a certain minimum standard of education was required. But I suppose all that has gone by the board now.'

Ghote declined the challenge.

'I was asking about your son,' he said firmly.

'Yes, you were asking. And I was answering. And you have heard my answer, so now go.'

'I have not yet heard your answer.'

'I have said. My son no longer exists.'

'And I am asking: what exactly do those words mean?'

'I was once a schoolmaster, as perhaps you know. And in those days I was quite prepared to explain to dunderheads the meaning of the simplest sentences. Now, however, I am retired, and I must be allowed some indulgence in my old age.'

'Sir, that is not adequate answer.'

'But that is all the answer you will get.'

'Sir, I would be most reluctant to invoke Section 179 of Indian Penal Code, refusing to answer a public servant authorized to question, but if necessary I shall do so.'

'I tell you, young man, I have answered. Are you deaf also?'

Ghote looked down at the little old man. He was standing ramrod stiff, glaring up at him, obdurate as a stone.

Was there any way of breaking such an object? Certainly nothing within the regulations he felt himself obliged to act under.

'You are quite unwilling to assist?' he asked at last.

'I have assisted in every manner I am able.'

Sadly Ghote turned away. Behind him the narrow door of the house shut with a quickness that betrayed the relief of the thin old arms pushing it.

But he had kept it up to the last, Ghote reflected. Those final words 'in every manner I am able', they were just the same sort of answers the old man had produced all along, expressions designed to keep within the strict truth yet convey an untruth. And although they betrayed that the old man had something to conceal, what it was he was hiding remained locked impenetrably in his rib-marked chest.

For a long while Ghote stood with his back up against the narrow closed door, letting the words of the conversation go round and round in his head like a tree-rat on a treadle in a cage, convinced he was bound to get nowhere.

'Raw egg – broken in two – white allowed to escape – passing yolk from one half of shell to other – white is then whisked for ten minutes – half a pint of cold water is then added.'

Suddenly Ghote awoke to the fact that the words that seemed to have added themselves to the treadmill in his head were not simply figments of his own imagination. He was actually hearing them.

He looked round at the narrow street in real alarm. A brisk rivulet of muddy water was chuckling its way along the drain in front of him. Two dogs rolled over and fought some distance away. But there was no one else.

The beggar. The beggar had been muttering those words. Words in, of all languages, English. And moderately technical words, too.

With a shiver almost of disquiet, Ghote realized that in fact he had himself long ago heard the words, or something very like them. He would not have been able to repeat them if asked but, hearing them, they became again immediately familiar. They were the directions for making something called albumin-water. It was an antidote for arsenical poisoning, and had other uses such as providing an excellent source of swiftly digestible light nourishment. He had learnt about it during his training.

He stood up more straightly and squared his shoulders. A faint smile crept on to his lips.

He bent down and put his hand firmly on the slumped beggar's shoulder. A strong reek of alcohol assailed his nostrils.

'Hemu Adhikari,' he said, 'I require you as pathologist formerly attached to the hospital in this town to accompany me to the police-station for questioning in connection with the death of one Sarojini Savarkar.'

16

It proved in the event not such an easy matter to get the drink-sodden pathologist to the police-station, and it certainly became evident in the process that questioning him was going to be no easy matter.

The man was a wreck. That was all there was to be said about it.

Ghote's efforts to get him to his feet had quickly enough brought old Mr Adhikari back to his door, and in the course of a good deal of argument and shouting certain facts had emerged. It had become clear that Hemu Adhikari had been deeply depressed in his forced exile. His wife had died, his only son had run off and had never been heard of since. He had taken to drink. But when he had lost his pathologist's post in Nagaland he had not, as had been generally supposed, gradually drifted into a state of idiocy and then died unnoticed. He had, just before it was too late, travelled home and put himself under the protection of his old father.

His father had hidden him in the house as well as he could, but he had been unable to cure him of his addiction. And eventually he had taken to allowing this human wreck, who looked in many ways more like an old man than he did himself, to sit outside the house anywhere within call and sun himself and sleep. And sun himself and sleep he had, and every now and again he had woken and remembered what it was that had been the cause of his downfall.

So the mutterings about poison and its antidotes and scraps of pathology had become a regular feature of his existence, heralds generally of yet another drinking bout. The old man had tried depriving him completely of any means of getting hold of alcohol, but the grimly unpleasant sight of his worn-out son in the grip of delirium tremens had been too much for him and after only two experiments in sternness he had let things slide. At least the shambling creature who was part of his household had ceased to attract any attention and had been safe from any further persecution at the Chairman's hands.

Poor devil, Ghote thought, as at last they got the slumped form that had once been a skilled pathologist into a tonga and were about to set out for the police-station. Poor ramrod old devil, it must have been a nasty moment for him when the Chairman's messengers called and began asking about his son just before his own visit.

The tonga set out, with Ghote cycling slowly after it through the criss-crossed muddy streets of the town.

As Ghote rode he allowed himself to jump the necessary gap of time in which steps would have to be taken to get Hemu Adhikari fit to talk. But when he was . . . Then they were bound to learn exactly what had happened at the autopsy and exactly what steps had been taken about the vital evidence of the re-moved organs. It was even possible that they might discover that they were still in existence. And arsenic would be found in them as surely now as it would have been fifteen years before.

They had entered the main street now. Ghote began to pedal harder, overtook the quietly jogging tonga with its slumped burden and went ahead to the police-station.

By the time Hemu Adhikari had arrived two constables were waiting for him. They picked him up, each with a broad hand in an armpit, and swung him like a half-filled sack across the forecourt and inside. Ghote, watching the operation with pleasure, paid the tongawalla and ran across to go in. The sooner he could get to work the better.

But he was not to have the broken pathologist under his hands as soon as he had hoped.

Just inside the doors of the police-station a figure planted itself full in his path and, stopping short, he found himself look-ing down at the lean and leathery hair-sprouting face of the old outcaste woman who had last accosted him as he had returned earlier that morning from his successful attempt at getting hold of the concealed Ram Dhulup.

He began plucking away the two scrawny, feeble arms which were clutching at him.

'I have already told,' he said, 'if you want to see me you must apply at the desk.'

'Inspector Ghote, I cannot tell those men this.'

In his anxiety to get down to the cells where the constables were putting the wreck of Hemu Adhikari he scarcely heard what she was saying. He succeeded in getting one arm clear and turned his attention to the other, as yet no more than brusquely firm but feeling anger gathering inside himself ready to break out into violence which he later no doubt would regret.

'Take your hands off,' he snapped. 'I have important work.'

'Inspector Ghote, I am wishing to tell you his secret. The Municipal Chairman's secret.'

He unpicked the other arm, only to find the first hand was gripping his trouser leg with skinny tenacity.

And then what the crone was saying properly entered his head. He thought for a moment. Could she . . . ? What would she . . . ? No, it must only be some nonsense.

'You must tell the constables,' he said.

'Inspector Ghote, why did I have his picture?'

His mind flipped back to those disastrous first few minutes in the town. The collision with this frail collection of bones in his determined hurry to get down to work, and the ridiculous yet appalling coincidence of such a creature clutching a copy of *Time* magazine that contained his own name and the Chairman's photograph.

'What is it?' he asked, dropping his voice to little more than a whisper.

'You will hear?'

'Yes. Yes, I will hear.'

He glanced quickly round. The constable on duty at the desk was too far away to overhear if he kept his voice down. No one else was near.

'What is it then?' he asked.

'Inspector Ghote, he is my son.'

Ghote stared down at her in blank amazement.

This old creature? This woman of the outcaste community? But the Municipal Chairman was not only a flourishing figure – he was a Brahmin. That had been a major factor in his request to have his first wife's body burned at the ghats.

She must be mad.

He looked across to the constable at the desk with the intention of beckoning him over to lead her away. But the man was for the moment busy completing an entry in the big leather-bound book in front of him.

'After all these years I saw that picture,' the old woman went patteringly on. 'After so many years. But I knew that birthmark, like a hen it was. How could a mother forget?'

Was it possible? Was it just possible?

'You saw the picture in that American paper?' he asked. 'And you recognized that mark? I had thought it was in the shape of a boat.'

'A hen, Inspector Ghote, a hen. From the moment I first saw him I said "hen". And "hen" it stayed till he ran away from his widowed mother and I thought he was lost to me for ever.'

'But he is a Brahmin,' Ghote said in complete dismissal.

'No. No, he is not. He was born to me. Whatever he may say he is my son.'

Ghote remembered then what Superintendent Chavan had told him of the Chairman's origins, of how he had come to the town with nothing and of his story of having lost his parents and all the family possessions in some outbreak of violence between Hindu and Moslem. He had accepted it as unchallenged truth when the superintendent had told it to him, but so apparently had everyone else all along. Yet it was possible that it was a complete fabrication. Why not? It would be utterly typical of the man with whom he had come face to face if it was so. If ever anyone could break the barriers of caste, as people did from time to time even in old traditional places like this, if ever anyone could it was the Municipal Chairman.

He looked down at the piece of flotsam of humanity who claimed to be the man's mother.

'You have seen him?' he asked.

'Inspector Ghote, I did not dare.'

'But you have dared to see me and tell me this.'

'You are the police, Inspector Ghote. He is a badmash, from the time he was a child he was wicked in his heart. Would he have taken his old mother into his arms?'

For Ghote this was the final seal. She knew the man she had claimed was her son.

'You did right to tell me,' he said. 'I do not know what will happen in this town. But come back here once every day and ask for me, I will see you are not forgotten.'

'Inspector Ghote. Inspector Ghote.'

The toothless gums seemed to mutter the words like an invocation. The scrawny figure wrapped in the once gaudy sari now faded to utter drabness turned and scraped her way across the stone-floored entrance hall of the police-station and out into the heavy damp heat.

And she gave birth to that man, Ghote thought.

So it was some while – even longer than the interview with the old crone had taken – before Ghote went to the cell where the constables had put Hemu Adhikari and began doing what he could to get his story out of him.

He had found it necessary first to go quietly into Inspector Popatkar's office and think about what he had heard.

Vinayak Savarkar was not Vinayak Savarkar at all but the hardy child of an outcaste mother and heaven knows what father. It was a startling enough fact. But the more he considered it, the more he became convinced that it was no more than that.

It was a fact. It gave him a powerful glimpse inside the man he was here to pin down on a murder charge. But it did not otherwise affect the issue in the least.

He could hardly use his luckily acquired piece of secret knowledge as a hold over the Chairman. No one was going to let themselves be blackmailed into allowing a murder investigation against themselves when the means to hinder it was at their hand.

And so there it was. The heir to the old Chairman's power and money had not been really in a position to claim it. In Bombay perhaps a self-made man from nowhere could end by marrying the daughter of a Brahmin family who had moved out of their religion-directed sphere, but in a small town like this it was unthinkable. Yet it was no more than this, a fraud that hardly came within the ambit of the secular law. Just that.

Ghote got up from his unseeing contemplation of Inspector Popatkar's pick-pocketing chart and made his way along to the cells.

He found the former pathologist sitting on the ground against the wall of the cell that he had been put into, and apparently relapsed quite quickly into a state of somnolence after the sudden starts and sharp cries he had given during the time he had been got into the tonga outside his father's house and on the journey to the police-station.

Ghote crouched down beside him.

'Mr Adhikari,' he said quietly, 'you have much to tell me.'

The slumped and bloated figure by his side – Ghote had learnt from the father that his actual age was only forty-nine but even as close as this he looked sixty – did not acknowledge in any way that he was being spoken to.

'Mr Adhikari,' Ghote said a little more loudly.

There was still no sign of response.

Ghote put his mouth not far from the right ear of the sparsely-bearded owlish-looking face.

'Mr Adhikari!'

A tremor ran all the way across the slack-skinned cheek near him. But it was clearly an involuntary movement. There was not the least other sign that he had been heard.

So, Ghote thought, he is going to try that, is he?

Clearly it was no time for the method of violence. He moved round a little till he was able to sit beside the pathologist on the floor with his back, too, comfortably against the cell wall. This was going to be a long job.

When he felt himself to be quite physically comfortable he

150

began. In a voice which he calculated was bound to be heard
however fuzzy the head beside him, but in no way in loud
tones, he started talking. He recounted first the immediate
circumstances that had made it important for him to hear
Hemu Adhikari's evidence. He took his time. He did not
hesitate to go back over the same ground, if it was likely that he
could improve the clarity of what he was saying. And gradually
he came round to formulating a statement of why it was vital
that the pathologist should tell him all he knew.

He kept a watch out of the corner of his eye on the tell-
tale cheek of the bloated figure next to him, but he was not
really disappointed during this opening half-hour's session to
get no response at all, and when he had thoroughly gone into
every aspect of the immediate circumstances he heaved a long
sigh and began again with a larger account, going back this time
to his own arrival in the town.

He told, over and over again, how Vinayak Savarkar was
suspected of the murder of his first wife, Sarojini. He recounted
how he himself had arrived in the town – no mention of the egg-
box and the humiliation he had suffered through it – and how
he had gone through all the papers in connection with the previous investigation fifteen years before. He forbore, not without difficulty, from any mention at this stage of the town's
pathologist of those distant days.

He accounted carefully and minutely for what he had found
in those piles of papers, leaving aside for the time being the
mystery that appeared to surround the organs removed from
the deceased woman's body, and concentrating instead on the
suspicious circumstances that the Coroner's Committee gave
rise to. He was in the middle of telling the story of his first
failure to find Ram Dhulup, the Chairman's crippled pensioner,
when he heard a low droning snore from beside him.

Sharply he dug his elbow into the heavy form slouched so
near him.

'Vomiting, violent thirst, burning sensation in the throat,'
Hemu Adhikari jerked out loudly. 'Pains in the stomach, cramp
in the calves is occasionally experienced.'

For a moment Ghote had thought he was complaining of

symptoms himself, but then he recollected what old Mr Adhikari had told him. The drink-sodden mind beside him was
going back again to its old preoccupation, this time running
over distractedly the main symptoms of arsenical poisoning.

Ghote took fresh heart.

If the man was so weighed down by the thought of a poisoning by arsenic, then there must be something on his conscience.
And that something could only be another brick to add to his
own case.

'I was telling how in the course of my first investigation I
attempted to learn from one Ram Dhulup, formerly a dhobi
in this town ... '

The narrative went on and on. He left Ram Dhulup and
moved to his more successful encounter with Bhatu the basketmaker from which it had emerged that the late Mrs Savarkar
had certainly experienced the symptoms of arsenical poisoning.

And here Ghote decided that he would risk pressuring a
little.

'Yes,' he said, 'Bhatu described these symptoms to me. First
he told me she had much vomiting and great thirst, and soon
it seems she was suffering severe pains in the stomach. This
shortly was followed – '

From the corner of his eyes Ghote saw that Hemu Adhikari
was reacting. He was scrabbling at the floor beside him with
a practically nerveless hand. For a moment Ghote wondered
what he was trying to do. Then the hopeless hulk succeeded.
He pushed himself sideways, rolled suddenly and ended up
curled in a great fat ball a yard or so away along the wall of the
cell.

Wearily Ghote pushed himself to his feet, bent over the
soft-fleshed hulk and righted it. He made sure it would not
easily topple over again and that beneath the drooping, twitch-
ing eyelids the blurry eyes were actually open. And then he
began again.

'As I was saying, from my inquiries with this Bhatu – he
was a basketmaker, you remember – I came to the conclusion
that that Coroner's Committee had not been conducted strictly
in accordance with the correct principles.'

It was early in the afternoon when Ghote, who had started his day before dawn in order to catch Ram Dhulup at the Chairman's house and had gone without any midday meal so as to keep up his light but steady pressure on the wrecked pathologist and who was beginning to feel extremely nervy in consequence, realized that Hemu Adhikari's physical condition was changing.

The slobbering cheek beside him was becoming convulsed with twitches more frequently. Twice he had alerted himself because the hand nearest him had scrabbled a little at the floor, but on each occasion it seemed that the bloated figure was not really making an attempt to roll away and he had done nothing about it. But now he had to acknowledge that a definite restlessness had set in and that this was accompanied by the withdrawal of even that passive attention his story had been receiving.

There had been more muttering, too. Ghote had had scraps of the symptoms of arsenical poisoning twice, and once he had had a version of that extraordinary rigmarole about the preparation of albumin-water that had alerted him to Hemu Adhikari's presence at his father's house in the first place.

He had had some experience of alcoholics in the slums of Bombay, and, unless he was very much mistaken, he thought he now detected the onset of an attack of delirium tremens in consequence of the withdrawal of alcohol.

He let his recital lapse for a few moments. There was now no chance of the hulk beside him going to sleep. And he thought about what his course of action should be.

Really he knew he ought to summon a doctor. Hemu Adhikari was almost certainly going to need treatment. But treatment would take a long time, and time was precious. At present, certainly, as far as he knew the town was quiet and the fasting Swami up there at the ruined temple was apparently no longer succeeding, after the revelation of his family link with the Chairman, in stirring up the passions of the town. But the Sikh doctor had made it plain that the old holy man could at any moment enter the borders of death, and if that happened it was more than likely that the agitation would start up again.

And in those conditions what chance would there be of pursuing investigations?

Yet there was one way in which the onset of DTs could probably be averted. The wrecked man beside him could be given a drink.

Ghote had seen the wonderful effect this often had on a figure trembling and afraid, talking of pink monkeys and every form of animal life, vomiting and broken. The swift flow of alcohol in the bloodstream could within minutes put that man back into a semblance of humanity again.

He pushed himself sharply to his feet.

'Constable,' he called, 'there must be rum in the station first-aid box, bring it quickly if you please.'

Half an hour later Hemu Adhikari was sitting, not on the floor of the cell he had been put into, but on the wooden bench. Ghote, who while the revival process was taking place, had snatched a hasty meal, came back with his hopes once more high.

'Mr Adhikari,' he said to the still owlish-looking drunk, 'with your help I am going to see justice done.'

'Justice?'

Ghote's spirits shot further up. His man was talking.

'Yes,' he said. 'For too long justice has been thwarted here.'

'Very true.'

The man's speech was slurred, but it was clear enough. And it showed signs of a clear enough mind. Perhaps it would not be long before that evidence was pouring out.

Hemu Adhikari raised an only slightly trembling hand and put it on his forearm as he bent towards him. Then the fingers curled in a surprisingly hard grip.

'It your fault,' he slurred out.

'My fault?' Ghote said.

'It was you who kept it away from me so long.'

'Kept what away?'

'Kept what away? Kept what away?' Hemu Adhikari mimicked.

He giggled a little.

154

'Kept drink away,' he explained solemnly. 'Kept drink away from me. Where justice in that?'

It had been too good to be true. Of course drink was likely to have had this effect on him.

Patiently Ghote settled down to wheedle, cajole and explain away, putting off till a time he refused even to contemplate any further talk of the real object of his being there.

And Hemu Adhikari's new cockiness lasted every bit as long as Ghote had feared. The old drunk wandered round the cell. He was abusive. He was incontinent. He never even so much as once muttered a single word on the subject of arsenic and arsenical poisoning.

It was only, in fact, shortly after dusk that the effects of that one administration of rum began to wear off. But then at last the young-old man came home to the bench beside Ghote and folded his arms across his big belly in a curling-up attitude that harked back to his demeanour when they had first brought him in.

'Not feeling so good?' Ghote asked him.

He grunted miserably in answer.

'I think I can tell you what was the beginning of all your troubles,' Ghote suggested.

He detected a glint of response in the drunk's half-closed eyes.

'I think,' he said cautiously, 'that your troubles began when you were sent far away from this pleasant place to Nagaland where everything is different.'

'Nothing the same.'

Ghote was unable to repress a little flicker of excitement at this new acquiescence. Surely now the hunt was on.

He spent some little time musing aloud about how unpleasant it must be to be sent away from the familiar surroundings of a lifetime. And then, when this met with hums-and-haws of vague approval, he ventured a stage further.

'It is no secret too why you were posted away to that place,' he said.

The figure beside him was still, but listening.

'It was because the Municipal Chairman did not like you to be here,' Ghote said.

'No. No, no, no.'

The denial was not vigorous, but it depressed Ghote. Had all the hours of patient friendliness been worth nothing?

Hemu Adhikari slowly turned his flabby-skinned face towards him.

'No,' he said slurringly, 'not Municipal Chairman. Municipal Chairman is dead, been dead a long time. I heard that I heard that there.'

Light dawned on Ghote. Damn it, Adhikari had left the town when the old Chairman was still alive, even probably before Vinayak Savarkar had married the old man's jaw-crackingly ugly daughter.

He set to patiently to straighten out the misunderstanding. And patience was necessary. But eventually he had it established that it was the present Chairman who was to be blamed for Hemu Adhikari's woes.

The old drunk turned and looked at him with bleary and bloodshot eyes.

'I could tell you something about that man, about that Savarkar,' he said.

Ghote leaned forward. He hardly dared breathe.

'But no. No, I will not. Not a word.'

And from that, during the rest of a long and tiresome evening, Ghote was unable to budge him. He tried many ways. He talked with unending patience, gradually building up in this direction and that a picture in the pathologist's wreck of a mind of the situation as it was. But even when he was certain that he had laid it all out, that the Chairman was in all probability guilty of his wife's death, that he had to be brought to justice if only to stop his career in the town that had hurt many others as badly as it had hurt Adhikari himself, and that the evidence from that post-mortem of long ago was mysteriously unclear, even when all this had been established still Hemu Adhikari stubbornly clung to the silence in which years of misery had impressed on him lay his only safety.

At midnight exactly Ghote decided to put into effect a switch treatment that he had been considering for an hour or more. Abruptly he got up and ordered Adhikari to be taken to another cell, the one he himself had used to work in on his first night in the town, a cell removed from the others in the station and with solid walls all round and a door with only a peephole in it as opposed to the barred front walls in the main cell block.

Some long hours of absolutely solitary meditation might do more for the drunk now than any form of questioning.

Having seen the wreck lifted once more by two hefty constables and placed in his new quarters, and having given stringent instructions that on no account was he to be talked to or even to see a human face for more than a moment, Ghote retired to the friendly sanctuary of Inspector Popatkar's office, stretched himself on the floor and fell immediately into a deep sleep. It had been a long, long day.

He was woken within ten minutes.

The night duty sergeant was kneeling beside him and shaking him. The light in the office was on. Blinking dazedly, Ghote registered that the burly fellow thrusting his face anxiously into his own appeared considerably worried.

'Inspector Ghote, Inspector Ghote, wake up.'

'I am awake. What is it? What on earth is it?'

'Inspector, Dr Patil is here.'

Ghote had not the least idea who Dr Patil was. His uncomprehending expression must have shown it.

'Inspector, it is Dr Patil, the Medical Superintendent at the hospital.'

Ghote remembered then. Dr Patil, the Gujarati, had been decidedly helpful despite his probable links with the Chairman, when he had visited the hospital to see whether Mrs Savarkar's removed organs could possibly be traced there.

And now he saw that, hovering by the door of the office, there was the tall, dignified, smooth-faced, slightly balding person himself, even at this hour of the night wearing a tie.

Ghote scrambled to his feet.

'Dr Patil, forgive me. Is there something I can do for you?'

But what on earth could it be?

'I thought it advisable to insist on seeing you, Inspector,' Dr Patil said blandly. 'The fact of the matter is that I have just received some decidedly disquieting news.'

'News?'

'From the old river temple, Inspector. The Swami is dying.'

17

Bemused from the deep sleep he had been in, Inspector Ghote absorbed the words which the urbane Dr Patil had dropped into the pool of his tranquility.

The Swami was dying. If the medical men said so, there could be little doubt about it. It had always been obvious that for a man of his age going without food day after day put him constantly in danger of death. And now it was coming. Plainly some symptom must have manifested itself that indicated that, without emergency measures of some sort to introduce some nourishment to that fast-eroded frame, death would supervene very soon.

And when that death came . . . When he himself by his own stubborn insistence on carrying out his investigation had been responsible for the death of this venerated figure, then all hell would break loose. It would break loose earlier than that in fact. It would break loose as soon as the news that the Swami was coming to the end of his life got about the town.

Ghote groped for his watch and held it close to his still bleary eyes to find out what time it was.

Not yet half past midnight. Thank God for that. Though rumours might begin to spread and people might get out of their beds to voice their fury, it should mean that until daylight came there would not be too much trouble.

His thoughts turned to Hemu Adhikari. Should he go back to him at once and somehow force out of him what he knew?

He looked up, blinking, at the Medical Superintendent.

'It was good of you to come and tell me this, Doctor,' he said. 'Do you know if the news is yet common knowledge?'

'It can only be a matter of time,' Dr Patil replied, his blandly smooth face expressing a dignified anxiety. 'My doctors cannot conceal the true state of affairs from the Swami's disciples. And they will talk. They will consider it their duty to talk.'

'Thank you, thank you,' Ghote said, still confused.

'I will keep in touch, both with my men at the temple and

with you,' Dr Patil replied. But now I will bid you good night.'

'Yes, yes. Thank you again.'

Ghote began pacing about Inspector Popatkar's little office trying to make up his mind what to do. On the one hand there was this new and great urgency, but on the other hand he had carefully calculated that the right treatment for Adhikari just now, if he was to crack the wall of silence the fellow had thrown round himself, was to leave him profoundly alone for a good long stretch of time.

He paced and thought.

In a little the night sergeant came back from seeing Dr Patil out into the midnight street.

'Inspector, you are wanting the prisoner for more questioning?' he asked.

Ghote found his mind was made up.

'No,' he said. 'He must be left to stew. No one is to see him, Sergeant.'

'Very good, Inspector,' the sergeant said.

But his tone left it in no doubt that he wished his orders had been different.

Ghote went back to his temporary bed again, but not to sleep. He ached with tiredness, in his knees and the small of his back. But he achieved no more than uneasy dozing, do what he might. His head buzzed a little too, and he took aspirin for it at some stage of the night. But even this did not let him sleep and it was only just before dawn that he did at last succeed in getting deeply off for a few minutes, and what woke him then was the sound of shouting in the street outside.

He knew what it was even before he had ceased dreaming. It was the start of the protests.

He got up, showered to try to make himself feel fresh, dressed for want of anything else in the same mud-stained clothes he had worn all the day before and went to see what the situation was.

It could have been worse. There were only twenty or thirty people in the street outside and they were doing nothing to get past the four constables drawn up behind the whitewashed iron-piping barrier of the police-station forecourt. But this was still only just after dawn. What would the protests grow to as the day wore on?

A new sergeant was on duty at the desk and Ghote asked him if they had any news of the Swami.

'Oh yes, Inspector. We are sending a man out to the temple every half-hour – while we still can.'

'And there is nothing new?' Ghote asked, knowing what the answer would be.

'Nothing new, Inspector.'

Ghote went to secure himself some breakfast before going down to see how a night's lonely thought had affected Hemu Adhikari. He did not feel hungry but he knew it was his duty to eat while he could. In the course of the day ahead there might not be all that many opportunities for food.

Then, feeling his last hurriedly masticated, deplorably un-crisp puri descending slowly towards his stomach like a piece of wet leather, he went to tackle the drink-wrecked pathologist.

He decided to interrogate him where he was, in the single solitary detention cell, feeling it important to avoid the least chance of interruption. If he was to get the drink-sodden hulk talking it would probably be a hair-balance delicate operation and the shortest of breaks at the wrong time might well spoil the whole interrogation.

He took the key from the constable on duty and let himself into the cell. Hemu Adhikari was awake. He was sitting up on the cell bench, which was a good sign. But on the other hand he took no notice of the door opening and he was muttering to himself.

'Taken by mouth in all forms is readily absorbed – excreted in urine – fulminating poisoning may occur . . .'

It sounded like his arsenic phobia again. And that was not too good a sign. This alertness could well be the herald of another attack of DTs.

'Good morning, Mr Adhikari,' Ghote said loudly and clearly.

At last the bloodshot eyes rested on him briefly.

'Have you eaten?' Ghote asked in the same bright tone. 'Shall I send out for food? What would you like?'

'No food,' the slack-bellied alcoholic muttered, turning away.

Ghote wondered if he should not send for a reviving dose of rum straight away. But its effect was almost bound to dissipate the pangs of conscience which the lonely night had been intended to establish in the drunk's sodden mind.

Ghote went and sat down beside him.

'Now,' he said, 'I want you to tell everything that happened when you performed the autopsy on Mrs Sarojini Savarkar.'

'I cannot think of it.'

This was better than the day before. It was not a blank refusal.

'But, my friend, you have been thinking of it, isn't it? You have been thinking all the night?'

Hemu Adhikari answered only by a groan. But it was clearly an affirmative groan.

'Come, something went wrong, did it not?'

'Do not ask.'

So, Ghote thought, I am not going to get it just yet.

He settled himself down to do just what Hemu Adhikari had requested him not to do: to ask. He asked in various ways. He suggested different reasons for the pathologist telling him everything. He grew tougher. He relapsed into more extravagant friendship.

And he watched his man. He watched closely every minute, while taking great care not to let him see he was so interested.

Two factors emerged. The first was that the pathologist was plainly caught in a dilemma: he wanted to talk and he wanted as passionately not to have to. And the second was that with every passing quarter of an hour the fellow was getting nearer an attack of the DTs.

He grew increasingly restless, sliding himself awkwardly to and fro on the narrow bench worn smooth by a thousand criminals' haunches. His attacks of tremors increased until by half-way through the morning they were visible as a continuous shivering all over the grey stubbled cheeks and in the slack half-open lips. Cold sweats broke out too from time to time and then subsided, adding a new ingredient to the pungent smell from his sprawling body.

Nor was the smell helped by the increasing heat in the little cell. Ghote would have liked to have had the door propped open – there was not the least chance of this wreck being able to escape – but he feared the temptations to interruption from outside that this would bring and steeled himself to endure the odours within, however unpleasant. It would have helped had there been any showers of rain to bring down the outside temperature, but there were no signs of any now that he wanted them.

Rain would have had another useful effect, too. It would have quieted the protests outside the police-station. Although he had no direct reports, Ghote was afraid these were still going on. Indeed, at about the time the old pathologist's attacks of trembling became united into one continuous shiver Ghote thought he detected even in the seclusion of the cell outbursts of sound coming from the front of the station. Or perhaps from the rear.

Which would mean that the agitation had gone beyond the protest stage and that they were under attack once more.

But at least the Swami must be still alive. If they had news of the death, Ghote was certain, they would have come and interrupted him no matter what.

'Listen,' he said to the smelly figure beside him, laying his hand on an arm which he could feel trembling hard beneath its dirty shirt. 'Listen, I know almost everything. I need only a little more to have proof against him. I know his wife died with all the symptoms of arsenical poisoning. I know that he was the man who had most opportunity to administer arsenic. I know that he took active steps to secure the destruction of the evidence in the body. But to make the greater part of my case iron-hard I need actual evidence that arsenic was in the organs. And you have that, isn't it? Isn't it?'

'Nagaland,' the hulk beside him replied.

'Yes,' Ghote said. 'He was responsible for you being posted away to Nagaland. He believes that you died there. You can come back from the dead to see justice done.'

'The monkeys there, terrible, awful,' Hemu Adhikari muttered.

'Yes, yes, but the organs. What happened when you had removed them from the body? You did that I know.'

162

'Monkeys. Monkeys are here too. There, there.'

A wildly shaking hand pointed quaveringly to the far corner of the cell.

'No, no. There are no monkeys here. Look, I will go over to the corner and show you there is nothing.'

Patiently Ghote went through the business of crossing to the far corner of the little cell and routing round there to show there was not the least sign of animal life. Hemu Adhikari appeared reassured. He sat up a little more straightly.

But for how long would it be possible to go on convincing him such hallucinations were not real, Ghote wondered.

He went quickly back to the bench and resumed his cajoling talk.

It was a little after noon by the watch on his wrist, which he permitted himself to consult surreptitiously from time to time, when he thought he had at last succeeded in breaking one more barrier.

Quite suddenly the old drunk had turned to him and clutched him hard by the front of his shirt. A wave of disgusting breath, prescient of appalling vomit not far away, swirled out over him. He had to make a strong mental effort to fight back a desire to be sick himself.

'If I told,' the drunk said slobberingly, 'if I told, what would you do for me?'

It was the first time that the old wreck had seriously brought himself to consider the possibility of a confession.

And then, coming briskly and inexorably along the stone-floored corridor outside, there was the sound of footsteps.

Ghote willed them not to exist.

But the sound grew louder.

The Swami, Ghote thought. He has chosen this moment to die.

He thrust his face a quarter of an inch nearer Hemu Adhikari's.

'We will protect you,' he said with all the force of conviction he could muster. 'I give you my personal guarantee of protection.'

This would bring untold difficulties later, he knew. But he

163

could not let this chance slip by. He would have to extract a promise of aid from the Eminent Figure and make sure somehow it was kept. When all this was over – and it might be so soon – and he himself was safely back in Bombay.

'Now,' he said, 'tell me, where are those removed organs?'

'Raw egg broken in two – white allowed to escape – passing yolk from one half of shell to other . . . '

They were back to that.

A sharp knocking came on the door of the cell.

Ghote got up, stiff with weariness, crossed over to the door and opened it.

The duty sergeant from the outer office was there.

'Excuse me, Inspector,' he said. 'I did not want to interrupt you but – '

'The Swami? He has gone?' Ghote broke in.

'No, no, Inspector. Still alive as far as we know. But we can no longer get over to the temple. Pretty bad outside there now.'

'Then what in heaven's name is it?'

'There is a telephone call for you, Inspector. From Bombay. They would not give name, but I could tell it was someone bloody high up, Inspector, and I did not dare leave it.'

Ghote sighed.

'You were quite right, Sergeant.'

He looked over at Hemu Adhikari. And to his astonishment he saw that the slumped figure was actually making movements as if he wanted to come across to him. The eyes were wide, and inarticulate noises were emerging.

Could it be that he wanted to confess? Now? At this moment?

'Sergeant,' Ghote said in a hurried whisper, 'go back and tell them that you have my own personal instructions to take a message. Say that something that might put the crown on my whole case is happening now, at this very moment. Say I cannot come.'

The sergeant, excellent fellow, needed no more telling. He left at once and Ghote almost threw himself across the cell to the drunken pathologist.

'Yes?' he said. 'Yes? What is it? Tell.'

Hemu Adhikari clasped his hand in his trembling yet tight grasp.

'It was not right,' he said. 'I did not do my duty.'

Abruptly he ceased speaking and seemed to become more rigid.

'At the autopsy?' Ghote said. 'You did not do your duty at the autopsy? How did you neglect it? In what way?'

'I will tell,' the pathetic figure murmured. 'In a little. I must get my strength.'

Ghote gently released the grip on his hand and resumed his seat beside Adhikari. He put an arm reassuringly across the shivering shoulders and waited.

It was on the point of coming, the fact that would put the crown on his case. He felt certain of it.

After about five minutes during which twice the old drunk made visible efforts to begin speaking, Ghote again tried urging him.

'Now,' he said, 'you can tell now. Remember I know most of it. It is confirmation only I am needing. So, now, you were performing the autopsy, and you did something against your duty, isn't it? What was that thing?'

'He made me,' Adhikari said, speaking more clearly than at any time hitherto. 'He sent goondas. Already they broke one of my toes. And they said they would do worse. I promised.'

A colossal shudder shook the whole slobbery frame.

'Yes?' Ghote almost whispered. 'What did you promise to do?'

'I promised that when I had removed the organs – They have to be sent to the Chemical Examiner. In Bombay. We have not the facilities here. The town is small and often I have complained . . . '

'Yes, yes. I know the organs have to be sent to Bombay. But what did you do with them?'

'Nothing. No. Yes. No, I will tell. I was ordered – '

And at that moment a rain of knocks on the cell door battering obscurely at Ghote's ear for some time, finally penetrated. They seemed at that climax to have penetrated the foggy mind of Hemu Adhikari as well because he stopped dead in his narrative and looked at the door with an expression of pure consternation.

Ghote leapt up and flung the door open.

The sergeant was there.

'Inspector, I thought you had been attacked. I knocked and knocked.'

'Go away. Go now.'

Ghote swung round to the pathologist.

'Inspector,' the sergeant went on behind him, 'Inspector, I took the message but afterwards he insisted. He told me he would get me sacked from the force. He would get me gaoled. Inspector, I believe him. The call is in Inspector Popatkar's office. You must come.'

Ghote looked at the pathologist, who had been severely disconcerted by the interruption and was absolutely unlikely to pick up again from where he had got to. He turned back to the sergeant.

'All right, I understand,' he said. 'I will go.'

He ran all the way along to Inspector Popatkar's office.

There on the desk beside the waiting telephone receiver was a long and detailed message in the sergeant's clear but laborious handwriting. Ghote subjected this to one frizzling look to make sure it dealt with all his inquiries and then seized the receiver from the desk surface.

'Ghote here,' he barked, careless of all security.

'Ah, at last,' came the familiar, querulous, detestable voice of the Eminent Figure. 'Inspector, I cannot really be expected to give messages to underlings. This is a highly confidential matter, I would remind you.'

Able here in Inspector Popatkar's office to hear a great deal more clearly the shouting and the crashing of hurled stones from the rioters outside, Ghote had a short answer to this.

'Sir the matter is by no means confidential here, I would assure you.'

'That is as may be, Inspector. But I am not accustomed to deal with the lower echelons.'

'Sir, I am in middle of a crucial phase of an interrogation. Did the sergeant tell that?'

'Ah, yes, Inspector, what interrogation is this? The man said it was an alcoholic you were interrogating. What possible significance can such a person have to your inquiry?'

'Sir, any minute of delay now may mean hours more work. And, sir, the Swami here is dying. Already there is rioting in the streets. If he dies, sir, and I have found out nothing I do not think I will succeed ever.'

'That is all very well, but what progress exactly are you making? I must be kept informed.'

'I am making progress, sir, but – '

'Inspector, you will tell me now exactly what you are doing. I wish to hear a concrete example.'

Blackening rage erupted in Ghote's head.

'Oh, if you wish that,' he shouted, 'I can tell that I have found out that the Chairman is the true son of an outcaste woman from Nagpur side. But that is not getting the inquiry anywhere.'

'What is this? What is this?'

The distant voice had lost every trace of the querulous.

'I am saying, sir, that subject in question has as matter of fact been misrepresenting his origins of birth. An investigation of this sort does not go on without making discoveries.'

'You have proof of this, Inspector?' the voice excitedly asked.

'I can produce the mother, sir, but – '

'Then you may return to Bombay as soon as you like.'

18

Ghote stood there beside Inspector Popatkar's desk with the telephone receiver still clamped to his ear. He said nothing. He hardly thought. The impact of that single sentence 'Then you may return to Bombay as soon as you like' seemed to have deprived him of the power of rational reply. On the silent line the sound of another telephone ringing and ringing, though faint, could be distinctly heard.

At some hived-off level of his brain Ghote thought with furious impatience 'Why do they not answer?'

At the far end the Eminent Figure appeared not to wish to add to his remarks.

At last Ghote found words.

'Sir,' he said, 'my inquiries in the case of Sarojini Savarkar deceased are not yet completed.'

'A fig for Sarojini Savarkar deceased. Do you understand nothing, man? We have got him. We have well and truly got him now. In a town like that such a thing will break him into a thousand pieces. Thanks to you, Inspector, he can be swept away at a breath.'

'Sir, it is you who do not understand. I have made certain inquiries. From them it looks as if very soon there will be a case of murder ready to bring. I cannot let the investigation drop.'

'Listen to me, Inspector. You were sent out there to do a job. To break that man. You were sent by me as the most suitable instrument to hand. You have done that job: you will return to duty.'

'Sir,' said Inspector Ghote, 'it is my duty to complete my case.'

And he replaced the receiver on its rest.

For some moments afterwards he stood there thinking what it was he had done. He had antagonized a person who was hand-in-hand with every member of the State government, a person who had only to make the most casual request of a colleague such as the Minister for Police Affairs to have him flung violently out of the police force in two minutes. Yet he could not have done otherwise. He knew it. He knew that he would not have been able to live with the thought of abandoning a case of murder at the whim of a politician when the whole case was within hours of being satisfactorily completed. His whole reason for existence would have been crumbled up to fragments inside him.

And then a gleam of light broke. There was one thing that could prevent all this. And happily it was just the thing he had sworn that he would do. If he successfully brought his murder charge against the Chairman he could hardly be dismissed from the police afterwards. That alone would save him.

But he had to make his charge stick.

He strode over to the door of the office, flung it open and marched back to the cell where Hemu Adhikari awaited him.

But Hemu Adhikari was not awaiting him. Hemu Adhikari had met someone else first.

'The monkey, the monkey,' he was screaming as Ghote unlocked the cell door. 'Take him away. He would shake my hand. He would touch me. The monkey. The yellow monkey.'

Ghote left him attempting to fend off the hallucinatory beast and went to fetch help. Things had obviously got to a pitch he could not deal with on his own.

He cursed as he went. He had known that a break in the interrogation at that point was likely to be disastrous, but he had not expected it to be as disastrous as this. The man might even go on struggling in this lost world of his for days.

He was contemplating raiding the station first-aid supply for a massive dose of rum when he saw the Medical Superintendent from the hospital, Dr Patil. He was standing just beyond the entrance hall, looking for all his bland dignity a little lost.

The sight of him made up Ghote's mind.

'Doctor,' he called sharply. 'I wonder if you could give me some assistance, if you please.'

Dr Patil turned slowly.

'Ah, it is Inspector Ghote. I came to say that there is no change in the Swami's condition. Indeed, I had the greatest difficulty getting here at all. If one of Chavan's excellent sergeants had not spotted me and sent a few of his men out with lathis I would have had to abandon the attempt.'

'It is pretty bad out there, then?' Ghote asked.

'They are calling out all the time, and stones are being thrown quite freely,' Dr Patil answered. 'But what can I do for you, Inspector?'

Ghote told him, and found to his delight that the doctor was by no means above turning to and seeing what could be done to bring Hemu Adhikari to a reasonable state. A sortie to Dr Rao's dispensary next door was made under the personal direction of Superintendent Chavan, who for all his connection with the Chairman seemed more than willing to do anything to help that could be construed as being strictly police business. And when certain drugs had been safely brought back treatment was begun.

'I must warn you however,' Dr Patil said, rubbing his long-fingered hands together professionally, 'that this is likely to take quite some time.'

'How long?' Ghote asked dismally.

'That I cannot tell, my dear fellow. But several hours at the least.'

Superintendent Chavan, his uniform still wonderfully uncreased despite his having been out among the stone-throwing, took off the steel helmet he had worn and held it solemnly in front of his ample belly.

'Inspector,' he said to Ghote, 'in view of Dr Patil's observation it becomes necessary for me to tell you that I cannot guarantee to keep those people out of here if the Swami should die.'

Ghote looked at him in consternation.

'But, surely, Superintendent . . . It seems your men are in such good command of situation.'

'Up to now, yes. A first-class show, though I say it. But I do not think you have the necessary conception of what will happen when they are hearing the fatal news.'

'As bad as that?' Ghote said, finding his worst expectations were being doubled.

'As bad as can be,' the superintendent answered. 'They would fire the place, Inspector, I am convinced of it.'

'In that case,' Ghote said, hearing the words as if someone else was speaking them. 'In that case I shall go out immediately and try to persuade the Swami once more to desist from his fasting.'

Both the superintendent and Dr Patil looked at him in frank alarm. It was the superintendent who spoke first.

'Inspector, if they realize out there who you are, I think they would tear you limb from limb.'

'But will they realize?' Ghote asked, making a fierce effort not to grab at this offered lifeline.

The superintendent considered the matter.

'I think you may be right,' he concluded. 'With communications cut from Nagpur there have not been any newspapers that might have printed your photograph. And then you could take with you that box of sample eggs. You have it still?'

'Yes, I have it.'

But now Dr Patil proceeded to pile on yet more reasons for caution.

'You are a brave man, Inspector,' he said, 'but all the same is there any good reason for going to the Swami? He is a most obstinate individual. What can you say to him now you have not said before?'

And again Ghote was constrained to reject the plea, though a part of him cried out 'Relent, relent.'

'I think I have something new to put to him, Doctor. Certain circumstances have come into my knowledge that might influence him.'

Yet would the Swami abruptly switch round on learning that his protégé was not a Brahmin? By no means necessarily, Ghote felt. But he knew that he had to go and try any expedient while it existed.

'No,' he said, 'he must be forced to give way. That is all there is to it.'

But it was only after considerable discussion of ways and means that he was able to put his plan into action at all. Though it was possible for a respected figure in the town like Dr Patil to get into the police-station provided he was willing to take a few risks with flying stones, and though a quick foray to Dr Rao's shop had been practical, it was by no means easy to get somebody out unobserved.

Eventually however a plan was agreed. Ghote was to leave by the back way, His departure was to be covered by a squad of constables making a sortie as if to relieve pressure on the rear wall of the compound. He was to take an electric torch with him and to signal when he wanted to return, the letter G for Ghote in Morse, dash, dash, dot.

It was typical, Ghote thought, of Superintendent Chavan's all-round efficiency that he should have this last piece of information at his finger-tips.

So his departure, when at last it took place, was conducted in an altogether efficient manner.

Under the superintendent's direction a ramp was constructed out of old oil drums and planks at a chosen point in the compound wall, so that a concerted attack could be made on the besiegers. And, on a given signal, a detachment of the toughest constables, steel-helmeted, lathi-armed and with wire-mesh riot shields strapped to the left forearm, mounted the ramp at a double, dropped down on the far side, re-formed in close ranks and carried out a classic lathi-charge against the rioters in the lane, the long rods swinging and falling in almost unbroken rhythm.

They cleared the mud-thick little lane in no time. Ghote, dipping down behind their shoulder-to-shoulder ranks and darting at the right moment away up a narrow side-lane, holding his egg-box as if it were a treasure-chest he was bent on taking into hiding, could not repress a feeling of warmly pure delight at seeing a rule-book police procedure so well carried out.

But he had to store such thoughts away at the back of his mind. For the time being all his energies had to be concentrated on getting away from the police-station area without being identified as coming from it. He ran steadily, the egg-box tucked under his left arm now, the long torch the superintendent had lent him clasped in his right fist, and he kept a good look-out for the least sign of any knot of rioters. But only the most timorous had chosen to escape the lathi charge in this direction and none of them had stayed to see what was happening. Indeed, no one was out at all. Even the dogs had slunk to safety and Ghote ran between the low houses in the area to the rear of the police-station without seeing a soul for as much as ten minutes.

He had been given good and clear directions too before

leaving, and so when at the end of his long dash he allowed himself to halt and look about him, before walking out in the guise of a visiting salesman for Grofat chicken feed, he found he was already within striking distance of the river and the road to the ruined temple.

He set off at a good pace.

On the way he met only a handful of people coming towards him. There was one middle-aged woman wearing a garish sari and a determined expression, a carrier of tidings if ever there was one, though plainly with not much tidings to carry at present. And there were two youths sharing a very battered bicycle and laughing and joking to each other, who stopped their antics decidely abruptly when they saw him coming. But again the two of them showed clearly that the Swami was alive still, though he guessed that they were spies sent by the Chairman to see whether he had his trump card yet. Luckily they were both too occupied with keeping secret what they had been speaking about so loudly to pay him much real attention and he hurried on.

At the temple itself there were no more people than there had been on his last visit. There were the crippled beggars and there were a few elderly women disciples who apparently preferred staying on the spot to going to the town to make more public demonstrations of their devotion to the Swami. But no one else.

Ghote made his approach carefully nonetheless.

Inside he let his eyes get accustomed to the gloom and then made for the inner room where he had seen the Swami on his last visit. He went towards it on tiptoe. None of the bent old women, crackedly chanting prayers, offered to stop him.

He put his head round the doorway. In the dimmer greenish light he saw that the Swami was no longer sitting. Instead he had lain down, or more likely he had been laid down. His body, naked from above the waist, could be seen gaunt and ribby as a famine-stricken corpse. And indeed it was plain from the terribly laboured, painfully slow in-and-out of the breathing that the man was only a hair's-breadth away from being precisely this, a famine-struck corpse.

Beside him the Sikh doctor Ghote had met on his former visit was sitting on a camp stool, stethoscope still dangling on his blue shirt, white turban as clinically neat in its every fold as it had been before.

His white teeth flashed in his dark beard as he greeted Ghote with a silent smile of recognition.

Ghote went up to him even more elaborately on tiptoe than he had earlier.

'How is he?' he whispered.

The Sikh replied in a voice little lower than normal.

'It could be minutes,' he answered. 'Or hours. Not more. He's very weak. Hardly taking anything in even.'

'I could talk with him?' Ghote asked, dreading the answer.

The Sikh wagged his stiffly turbaned head.

'He would understand,' he answered. 'If you spoke loud, and kept things pretty clear. But I cannot vouch for what it would do to him.'

Ghote looked over the doctor's burly shoulder at the near-corpse on its pallet at the far side of the little room. He watched the ribs under their almost constricting covering of thin rubbery skin climb fraction by fraction upwards as a breath was taken in. He watched them cease from every movement at the apogee, and wondered whether they had at that very moment ceased from movement for ever. Then at last he saw them sink fraction by fraction downwards as the breath was expelled.

'He is so weak,' he said to the doctor, 'can you not feed him a little? Is there nothing he can have?'

'Oh, yes,' the Sikh answered, 'there are a variety of things that can be used for forcible feeding at such a time, and if one were administered with care it'd be pretty likely to do the trick. Orange juice, buttermilk, coconut juice, there are lots of suitable treatments.'

'Then why . . . ?'

'Not one of them in here, old boy. They won't trust me with them. Irreligious Sikh, you know.'

'They?'

'The old women out there. They've got something ready though, and if I come out and tell them he's willing to take it they'll be in in a jiffy and let me give it to him. But only after he's made it quite clear he wants it.'

'Cannot you go and take it from them by force?' Ghote asked.

The Sikh grinned.

'More than my life's worth once it got out, old boy,' he said.

Ghote fell silent.

But only for a moment. An idea, a wonderful, monstrous idea had come to him.

He looked up at the bushily bearded Sikh calculatingly, and then he began.

'Listen, if it so happened that some nourishing substance had been left in here, or had got into here, without those old women having any idea at all about it. Would you take it on yourself to administer in those circumstances?'

'What's this, old boy, moral debating?'

'No,' said Ghote, taking the egg-box from under his arm and flipping it open in front of the Sikh's astonished eyes. 'It is not joking. It is fact.'

It seemed like two whole minutes at least while the doctor stood there looking down at the box with its dozen, enormously large, grease-preserved eggs nestling inside it.

Then at last he spoke.

'Give me a hand, old boy, and we'll have something in him in a jiffy. We'd better mix it with a bit of water, digests easier that way. And I'm allowed a chatthi in here for hygienic purposes.'

'Yes,' said Ghote, a gleam in his eyes. 'You take a raw egg, break it in two, allow the white to escape by passing the yolk from one half of the shell to the other and the white is then whisked for ten minutes, and half a pint of water is added.'

The Sikh looked at him, his eyes widening.

'Albumin-water,' he said. 'How on earth did you know that?'

'It was one of the pieces of information I had to learn at detective school,' Ghote answered. 'And, God forgive me, I thought it useless only then. But just recently, as it so happened, I was reminded of it.'

175

'Well,' said the Sikh, 'you'd better crack the egg then. Look, here's a little lota, we'll whisk it in that. But not for as much as ten minutes. My nerves wouldn't stand it.'

He picked up the small brass pot and held it between his broad palms.

Ghote selected the biggest of the big eggs from the box. He took it between the first two fingers and the thumb of his right hand and with one sharp tap on the edge of the pot he broke it.

The Sikh plunged his bearded face downwards and sniffed.

'Smells fresh enough to me,' he said.

In heart-pounding excitement Ghote juggled with the two halves of the broken eggshell, plopping the pale yellow yolk from one to another, allowing the sticky white to trail in long tapering drains into the little brass lota.

Quite soon it was done. The Sikh dipped the tip of his stethoscope into the fluid and whirled it vigorously around.

'Not just what our wives would use, old man. But it'll serve.'

And a few minutes later – they had stopped the whisking by mutual consent – they were adding a stream of water from the earthenware chatthi to the froth the Sikh had created. He swirled the lota round a little.

'Should do,' he said. 'Let's try. You keep a look-out. I'll administer.'

Ghote darted across to the low doorway and peered out. The praying old women were praying still. He drew into the shadow and watched them. Behind he could hear faint sounds from the Swami's pallet – murmurs of encouragement from the Sikh, the tiny chink of teeth against the edge of the brass lota.

And then he heard the Sikh's heavy breathing being deliberately retained while he put the stethoscope – 'Clean handkerchief, thank God' Ghote heard him murmur as he wiped it – to the fasting man's chest.

The examination took a long time. But at the end came the voice of the doctor again, incredibly robust.

'Well, that went down all right. Got to wait a bit of course. But I'll bet my best scalpel he'll rally round all right now,'

19

Ghote waited an hour more in the temple and by the end of that time he was able to see for himself that there was a clear improvement in the Swami's condition.

So he set off for the police-station again with the comfortable feeling under his belt that at the very worst he had gained a good length of time. If all went well over the last push, he dared to think, he would have the Chairman in gaol awaiting trial before the beneficial effects of the albumin-water ceased to sustain the Swami any longer.

And, examine his conscience how he would, he could not really find any trace of remorse over the violence he and his cheerful accomplice had done to the old man's beliefs. After all, the Swami had been attempting to gain his ends by taking a life, even though it was his own. All he himself had done was to use equally strong counter-measures. And they had saved the old man and there was nothing that could be done about that now.

And when he reached the area at the rear of the police-station he found that, thanks perhaps to advance notice of the improvement in the holy man's state, or thanks simply to the fall of darkness, the attack on the compound wall had melted away. There was no one about in the lane, and, although he gave his torch signal as in duty bound, there was really no need for it.

So within half an hour of leaving the temple he was confronting Dr Patil once more and inquiring about the state of another patient.

'Yes, Inspector,' the bland-faced doctor replied, 'we have had some success. I think I can say that. More success, indeed, than we might have done.'

'Then I can resume my interrogation?'

Dr Patil raised a dignified arresting hand.

'Oh no, no. My dear sir, I did not say that.'

'But you told you had had success.'

'Yes, indeed. Success we have had. But the treatment must

be allowed to take its full course. Tomorrow morning perhaps . . . '

'I regret then, Doctor,' Ghote said with unaccustomed hostility, 'but I shall have to see the prisoner and form my own judgement. Such a long delay is inadmissible.'

Dr Patil looked offended from the tips of his well-polished black shoes to the crown of his domed and balding head.

'Very well, Inspector,' he said, 'if there is so much urgency, then perhaps you could take a risk and resume your questioning at . . . '

He paused and consulted his gold-banded wrist-watch at solemn length.

' . . . at, shall we say, midnight.'

'Thank you,' Ghote said stiffly.

So it was a few minutes after midnight that night, when Dr Patil had re-examined Hemu Adhikari and had somewhat reluctantly agreed, that provided he himself was on hand, the pathologist might be fit for questioning, that Ghote got down to work again.

He found, however, that he was tackling an altogether different figure both from the man at the mercy of the yellow monkey he had come back to after his terrible telephone call from Bombay and also from the alcohol-bemused creature he had originally tried to get some sense out of. Dr Patil's treatment had been every bit as succesful as the tall Gujarati had claimed: Hemu Adhikari was a changed man, alive, alert, aware.

It came out in his answer to Ghote's first cautious question.

'You remember what we were talking about before?'

'I remember nothing, Inspector Ghote. Why are you keeping me here?'

'So you know my name?' Ghote said, when he had recovered from the unexpectedness of it.

'Yes, I know your name, and I know also why you are here. And since I can in no way help you I am asking why you are keeping me in this cell.'

'I am keeping you here because I believe that you can help me.'

178

'You will find not.'

And for a long time it looked, indeed, as if Ghote would find not. He kept pegging away at the pathologist as he had done before, but this time the man fought back. He fought back like a piece of resilient rubber, pushing outwards every time Ghote pushed in and ending always just where he had been before.

Once again Ghote went over every aspect of his case against the Municipal Chairman, looking for the least opening in the rubbery armour of the man in front of him. He told him in so many words that he could prove that the Chairman had manipulated the Coroner's Committee so that, not only would its members bring in a verdict that meant that no action need be taken, but also that the body, the main piece of evidence for the poisoning having taken place, would be conveniently destroyed.

Hemu Adhikari, still fat with the effects of much drinking but with a skin that no longer hung too slackly from the folds of his flesh, constantly asked what it all had to do with him, constantly pressed to be allowed to go free.

Ghote was constrained simply to pretend the words had not been said. He tried a new tack.

'Very well, perhaps the proceedings of the Coroner's Committee were not your direct concern. But something else was.'

He darted a quick look at the pathologist.

'Inspector,' Adhikari replied with brightness, 'all this was many years ago and I will remember nothing.'

'You will remember performing the first stages of an autopsy on the body of one Sarojini Savarkar.'

'No, Inspector. Many, many such autopsies I have performed. How can I remember one from another?'

'You remember this because of what you were asked to do with the organs you had removed to send to the Chemical Examiner in Bombay. You told with your own words yesterday.'

'I told? Inspector, then I was ill. I did not know what I was saying.'

With flogged-on patience, Ghote went on to his next area of attack.

'Do you know that on the day that man's wife died he returned from a sudden trip to Bombay?'

'Inspector, what have I to do with trips to Bombay?'

'Because if a man in this town was wishing to acquire a supply of arsenic then he would do well to go to Bombay where such things may be obtained at cheap dispensaries in the suburbs with no one to ask questions.'

'If you say it is so, I will believe you. But all the same it is nothing to do with me.'

'It is to do with you. I have reason to believe that the arsenic obtained that day was administered that evening and that you were the one who removed the organs in which the substance was contained, and still would be contained today.'

'Inspector, there are records up at the hospital. If you wish to know what happened to those organs you have only to consult.'

'I have consulted. The arrival of the body for dissection is there, and its departure under an order from the Coroner's Committee is noted also. Nothing is noted about the dispatch of the organs.'

'Often such records are incomplete.'

'You were a most conscientious keeper of records. I have the Medical Superintendent's word for that.'

'Then for once I must have made a mistake. It is so long ago I cannot possibly remember.'

'I think you remember well what you did with those organs.'

'Inspector, after fifteen years.'

'I think also that those organs are still at the hospital. There are many jars of such things stored there, even some with no labels or with labels with numbers on only. I think those organs are among them still. You were a man, they told me, who was always writing letters but not sending. I think that with those organs you did the same. They are still at the hospital, isn't it?'

Hemu Adhikari shrugged his well-fleshed shoulders.

'Inspector, it may be so.'

'Ah.'

Ghote pounced.

'Now where are they? Tell, tell. You have only to tell and I will give you again the assurance I have given already: you will come to no harm in this town.'

'Inspector, I am saying it may be so because I cannot tell otherwise. It is fifteen years since I have been in that hospital. How can I know what is there or not there?'

And he had the impudence to smile.

But Ghote restrained his violent desire to take the fellow and trounce him as he deserved. There might still be a chink in this armour of his, and that would not be found by battering. The time for violence would come when other hopes had been exhausted.

The night wore on. Ghote kept up his questions. Adhikari kept up his rubber-bouncing replies. And of the two, Ghote suspected he himself was becoming the more tired.

'When it comes to prosecution,' he said at some stage, wearily hunting for the words, 'police will have no difficulty in showing motive. We are going to have cast-iron case, make no mistake about that, if you please.'

'Whatever case you have, Inspector, it will be case without me.'

'It is not so much you,' Ghote replied, searching for a quarter inch of leverage somewhere. 'It is not so much you. It is the material evidence of the organs. They exist still, isn't it? Isn't it?'

'Inspector, how can you expect me to know? All those events were so long ago.'

'Yes,' Ghote said, 'those events were in the past, but there will be events in the future also. I ask you to think of them.'

'In the future?'

Adhikari looked a little upset at this new line Ghote had hit on.

'Yes, in the future,' Ghote pressed quickly in. 'Let me show you a little of the future in this town. In a few minutes from now you are going to give me the information I want. It will be almost the last item my case needs. And when that case is complete to my satisfaction I shall make arrest.'

He delivered the words with all the force he could bring to

them. But he had to acknowledge that so far he was making no impression.

He resumed.

'And what follows that arrest? Oh, a great deal of legal palaver, of course. A great many attempts to suborn witnesses, to show that I myself am corrupt, to obtain bail. A hundred and one things. But they will all fail. And do you know why?'

'Inspector, all that will be of no interest to me.'

'I will tell why. Because when the people here see their Chairman is behind bars all the support for him will melt away. And it will have somewhere to run to, I can assure you of that. A certain eminent figure in State Politics is waiting only for his chance to take over here. One weakness from the Chairman and the tide will turn one hundred per cent.'

Ghote looked hard at the swollen figure beside him. Was this prospect he was holding out, of a town no longer dominated by the flashing crocodile grin of Vinayak Savarkar, was it opening new horizons for this man?

It seemed not, although his expression was at least no longer actively opposed.

Stolidly Ghote set out to paint in the details of his imagined new world.

'Yes,' he said, 'there will be a new set-up in the town altogether. It will mean many changes. That ugly daughter of the former Chairman – you knew her? – she will no longer as Chairman's wife be laying down the law to all the ladies of the district. And her son – '

He thought suddenly, not of the idealized picture he was painting for the purpose of transplanting Hemu Adhikari into a clime where a confession of his past misdemeanour would seem an easy matter, but of the real Vasant Savarkar, aged fourteen and condemned to marry no doubt for strictly dynastic reasons.

'Did you know the Chairman had a son called Vasant, a boy on the threshold of manhood?' he asked the fat pathologist.

'What is such a boy to me?'

'To you, nothing perhaps. But he is a person in this town, and his life will be very much changed by what is going to happen. He will not have to marry a girl who has already been picked out for him, he will lead a life of comparative poverty but one day he will come to marry some other girl, one perhaps more suitable, and then he will live out the rest of his days the way we all do, rubbing along from bad to better.'

'Inspector, all this is nothing to me.'

'No,' said Ghote, 'but to me it is something, a little. The lives of all the people I have encountered here in this town are something to me. Yours also.'

But the pathologist was still not to be lured by friendship, even though genuine.

'Inspector, you will go away soon. Perhaps tomorrow and everything here will be as it always has been.'

'No,' Ghote almost shouted. 'No, it will not. I told already at some time in this night that the Chairman is not the Brahmin everyone here has taken him for. Did I not?'

'Inspector, such things will not be believed when it is a rich and powerful man they are said against.'

'I could bring his outcaste mother to this very cell to show you,' Ghote countered. 'Perhaps she will end her days greeting her broken son as he comes out of prison, though that will be many years from now.'

'Inspector Ghote, men like the present Municipal Chairman do not go to prison.'

'Why do they not?' Ghote retorted, with his confidence growing as he began to believe his own vision of the future. 'Why do such scoundrels not meet their just deserts? Do you think it is because they have holy men to fast to death for them?'

A sheer clarion call of triumph sounded in his mind.

'I tell you,' he harangued the obstinate alcoholic, 'the Swami who was fasting against my investigation into this crime has eaten. He has taken white-of-egg and water. A most nourishing preparation, as you well know. He has taken that. Now, will you also take your medicine? Will you tell me what exactly you did wrong at that autopsy?'

The pathologist held his face without moving a muscle.

Ghote crowded in any fact he could get to hand.

'All will be different in this town, I tell you. Others will have

183

nothing to fear, and you need not. There is the man Ram Dhulup I told you of. He too committed a crime at the Chairman's behest. He gave the Coroner's Committee information about the deceased's religious beliefs that he knew to be false. Will he be prosecuted? No. He will live in peace. Certainly he will lose the pension he has been receiving all these years. But he will also lose the wife who would have made the rest of his days a misery. Ram Dhulup will be the happier for the Chairman's departure. So will you also.'

A smile appeared on the pathologist's drink-bloated face.

Was this in anticipation of his rosy future?

'Inspector,' he said, 'you are talking nonsense only.'

Ghote faltered.

'But Bhatu,' he stammered. 'But Bhatu the basket-maker. Did I tell you about him? He too will be happy here in this town. The threat that has hung over him, little though he knew it, will be gone. He will live to a contented old age.'

'Inspector, you are telling tales and no more.'

'No. You too will end your days in peace. No need to hide in the fumes of alcohol when there is nothing to hide from. Once more your old father will be able to be proud of his son. You will work again even.'

'No, Inspector Ghote.'

'Yes, yes, yes, I tell you.'

But all Ghote's conviction could not penetrate the hard layer of caution that the years had grown on to Hemu Adhikari. And at last he realised that he had tried everything there was to get the tiniest leverage into the minutest crack somewhere.

The time had come for the method of last resort. Probing and patience had failed: it was the hour for violence.

He leapt suddenly and sharply to his feet. He swirled round and glared down with red ferocity at the fat man.

'Shall I tell you what you are?' he shouted, leaning deliberately forward so that the spittle from his mouth sprayed on to the grey-stubbled face in front of him.

He watched it land, watched it with pleasure. And he saw too that in the man's eyes – so much less bloodshot after Dr Patil's ministrations – a look of sudden fear had appeared.

'No? No?' he shouted at him. 'You do not want to hear what you are? I know very well that you do not. Because you could not bear it.'

He felt the rage he had allowed himself at last to release sweeping through his head like a scouring tide.

'But I am telling you what you are. You are murderer.'

The old face in front of him had begun to tremble again as it had trembled when he had first put questions to it. Then he had tried to stop that shivering: now he rejoiced in it.

'Yes, murderer, murderer, murderer,' he yelled. 'You are refusing to bring to justice a man who has killed, who has poisoned. You and you alone could do it. And you refuse. I am telling you what you are: you are a murderer just as much as if you had given that arsenic with your own hand.'

He put such venom into the word 'arsenic' that it might have been a whip he was cracking down across the trembling face in front of him. And he saw the blow land. He watched the word sinking in, going deep into the brain. He saw the fight not to let it hurt, the struggle to achieve stoniness.

There was a time – a space of seconds that could be counted – when it looked as though the fight to maintain indifference was going to be won. Things hung in the balance.

And then tipped.

One great, gulping, wrenching sob shook the heavy frame of the man cowering on the bench. It was like the breaking of a dam.

'Yes. Yes. I will tell.'

It was definite, irrevocable.

Ghote knew there was no hurry now. The break had come, and it had been a decision taken in sober blood. It would not be gone back on as the other had been.

He stepped a pace away and stretched himself luxuriously.

'I think we will go somewhere else,' he said. 'We will go to the office I have been lent here. It would be more convenient for the taking down of the statement.'

The old man on the bench was crying quietly now, a long stream of tears slowly being released after the pent years. Ghote raised him up by the elbow and led him out of the cell.

He looked about for the night sergeant or someone equally competent to witness the recording of the statement. And he spotted somebody even better than he had hoped. Superintendent Chavan was sitting at the end of the corridor from the solitary confinement cell, talking to the indefatigable Dr Patil who had been stretching his legs on a hard chair waiting in case his patient was not able to stand the strain of a long interrogation.

He jumped up with an anxious look when he saw Ghote solicitously helping the broken-bodied pathologist along towards them. But Ghote got in first.

'Superintendent,' he said briskly to Chavan, 'I am just going to take statement. Would you be good enough to act as witness?'

The superintendent, uniform with every crease in place even at this late hour of night, looked suddenly delighted. Ghote realized that, for all the man's allegiance to the Chairman, what counted with him first was the routines of his calling and here he was being offered one of the most satisfying moments of such routines, the achievement of confession to a criminal act. And, Ghote thought with pleasure, perhaps in the years to come fewer pressures would be put on this colleague of his and he would be able to do his duty unmolested.

So it was a small triumphal procession that went along, not to Inspector Popatkar's office but to that of the superintendent himself to hear in full the confession of Hemu Adhikari.

And it turned out that the supposition that Ghote had put to the pathologist as a means of extracting perhaps a denial, perhaps a part-admission, was the exact truth. The man who had written letters of complaint to drug-manufacturers by the score and had yet lacked the final impetus to send them had done just exactly the same thing with the organs he had removed from the body of Sarojini Savarkar. Her husband had sent his men to frighten him into destroying them, but he had been frightened of doing that too. So he had compromised: he had put them in a jar of preservative and he had filled the jar with a number only on the label.

At this point the superintendent, solicitous still perhaps for his friend and patron, broke in.

'You put number only on the jar? Then how after all this time can you remember what number that was?'

'Sir, it was the figures of my birth date. How shall I forget that?'

It was then that Ghote picked up the telephone and got through to the hospital. A voice he thought he knew answered boomingly.

'Night-duty doctor. Hello.'

'It is you, Doctor – Doctor – '

He realized he had never known the cheerful Sikh's name. But Dr Patil had recognized the loud tones.

'It is Dr Surinder Singh,' he supplied tactfully.

'Dr Surinder Singh? Inspector Ghote here.'

'My friend. What can I do for you, old boy?'

Ghote told him as concisely as he could exactly what he wanted. There was a pause while the doctor went away and made his investigations. It was not a very long pause. Then came the breezy voice on the other end of the line.

'Ghote?'

'Yes? Yes?'

'You're quite right, old boy. Bottle there, just where you said. Label still firmly adhering. Figures exact. And the contents appear to be . . . Just a minute. Ah, yes. One stomach, one duodenum and the best part of one jejunum. Very neatly dealt with, too.'

'Thank you, Doctor. Would you be kind enough to impound the bottle until I can fetch it in the morning?'

'Certainly, old boy. I'll pop it in the poisons-cupboard. No one goes there except under my personal eye at this time of night.'

'That sounds excellent, Doctor. Good night then.'

'Good night.'

Ghote put down the receiver and turned to the others.

'Yes,' he said, 'it is there. Intact.'

'Very good, very good indeed, Inspector,' Superintendent Chavan said, his eyes shining with sheer policemanly pride.

And then, visible to see, another side of him took over.

He coughed.

'However,' he added, 'I feel it is necessary to point out that the mere discovery of organs which we cannot doubt were removed from the body of the late Mrs Sarojini Savarkar, and which we can even concede are certain to be found to contain arsenic, that these do not constitute a sure and certain case against any person. Or persons.'

'No,' Ghote admitted, 'they do not. I have shown that the victim died of arsenical poisoning. I think anyone would be prepared to admit that the Municipal Chairman of this town was a man who had a strong motive for murdering his then wife, but –'

'But,' Superintendent Chavan burst in, 'you have still to show that the Chairman ever obtained such arsenic.'

'He obtained it in Bombay.'

It was the voice of the pathologist, an almost forgotten figure since he had made his confession. But now, all shaking and bright-eyed, he was plainly intent on hammering every nail that could be got hold of into the coffin of the man he had at last dared to betray.

The superintendent bent on him a glance compounded of shock and distaste. It was no proper thing for an accomplice-after-the-fact to attempt to take part in the investigation.

Ghote hurriedly intervened.

'Yes,' he said. 'The arsenic was obtained in Bombay.'

'But you must prove it,' Superintendent Chavan said. 'You must prove your accused actually made the purchase in question.'

'I can,' Ghote said.

The superintendent looked at him with his mouth positively falling open.

'You can prove?'

'Yes. I knew always that the best place for such a man as the Chairman to obtain arsenic was at some small run-down dispensary in some suburb of Bombay, and when I learnt that very shortly after the crime was committed a Gujarati was appointed from nowhere to be Medical Superintendent in a town so distant from his native place as this, and having heard the Chairman boast that every post including that of a boss at the hospital was in his giving, I did not have far to look.'

He swung round and confronted the bland, dignified Dr Patil.

'You told me yourself that you came from the Bombay Gujarati suburb of Walkeshwar, Doctor,' he said. 'That was where I requested investigations to be made. I had a telephone message from Bombay this afternoon saying that they had been successful.'

They had only to see the visible collapse on the Medical Superintendent's habitually egg-smooth face to know that the case against the Municipal Chairman was complete. Savarkar had obtained the arsenic, he had had clear opportunity to administer it and it could be proved beyond shadow of doubt that it was arsenic that had been administered.

Inspector Ghote had broken through.